TWISTED LIES 3

SEDONA VENEZ

"Love all, trust a few, do wrong to none."
—**William Shakespeare**

CORE

MY LONG STRIDES covered the short distance from the curb to the entrance. Reaching for the door, I swung it open and entered the expansive lobby of my pet project, the McKay Club. Employees scampered about, efficiently cleaning and scrutinizing every aspect of the interior in preparation for tomorrow night's opening.

"Hello, Mr. McKay," they greeted in unison before resuming their tasks.

The rich and famous were notoriously hard to please, and I made sure the McKay Club over-delivered with a one-of-a-kind kinky spectacle. It was what kept the voracious patrons coming back for more. From upper crust to celebrities, all would clamor to get on the waiting list just to party on the rooftop terrace of the club. But the real lure of the McKay Club was the Noire lounge—a private, members-only playground where the well-heeled indulged in discreet sexual fantasies.

After walking across the lobby, I pulled back the expensive fabric draped over Noire's entrance, stepping over the threshold. Advancing down the mirror-ceilinged staircase leading to the lounge, I smiled just thinking about how close I was to finally destroying Bigsby Calhoune by stripping away everything he held dear—his wealth, freedom, political career, and trophy fiancée, Cate.

But why is the taste of revenge suddenly so bittersweet on my tongue?

The vision of Sinthia's eyes dilated with lust flashed in my mind. Basic, raw hunger surged through me, beating at my self-control. Sin was everything I wanted in a woman—strong and feisty. The idea of fighting to have Sin submit to me had my cock throbbing and my balls aching.

Damn. My fixation on her was annoying, cloying, and a complication I didn't need. Sin was bait, a casualty in my war against Bigsby.

But I knew I was fucked the moment she swayed onto the rooftop. I'd seen the fire and determination in her eyes, and my cock had gotten hard.

Damn, I loved it.

Her body had moved like a panther—sexy, driven, and confident. She was tall and voluptuous with curves that cried out to be caressed. In a matter of minutes, she'd shattered my control. It had taken every bit of self-restraint not to pull up her dress and fuck the shit out of her.

Shit. How the hell did I let it go so far?

The smoldering lust between us was already out of control. I wanted her in my bed so I could fuck her in every dirty position possible.

My cell rang, interrupting my dark thoughts. I didn't recognize the number.

"Yes?" I answered gruffly.

"Core, it's Tabitha."

What the fuck? I stopped mid-stride. "How did you get my private number?" I snapped. "You know what? I don't give a shit. Lose it." I was seconds away from disconnecting.

"Wait! Don't hang up. I need more money," she shouted urgently.

"Hell no," I barked.

"You don't get to say no."

The muscles in my shoulders bunched. "Are you threatening me?"

I didn't respond well to threats, especially from a money-hungry whore like Tabitha Thorp, who had served her purpose when I recruited her to help me get close to Sin. Tabitha had convinced Sin of the value of getting an investor—specifically, me—to help her expand her business. In exchange, I'd agreed to pay off Tabitha's debt to Ben Vargos, her unsavory criminal ex-boyfriend, and send her on a very long vacation.

"It's not a threat. Just a statement. You owe me," she snapped.

My lips flattened. "I don't owe you shit. I paid you five figures in cash to make the Sin deal happen."

"It wasn't enough!" she exclaimed in a rushed tone. "I ran into a few bumps, and now I'm broke. You're the only person I can turn to right now."

"Go fuck yourself, Tabitha. Our business was done the moment you took my money."

I knew Tabitha from the old neighborhood. When we were young, we hung out in the same criminal circles. The only difference was, back then, the now-famous Tabitha had worked as a drug mule for her seedy kingpin boyfriend, Ben. I'd even fucked her several times behind Ben's back.

"One call to Sin and..." Tabitha trailed off deliberately.

I replied with deadly intent. "If you even think about—"

She sputtered with a whiny voice, "I'm not one of your whores. I'll tell her you blackmailed me into betraying her."

"I didn't twist your arm to take the money. And the recording of our business arrangement will surely enlighten Sin." I continued moving toward the elevator.

Tabitha gasped. "What recording?"

My nostrils flared. "Do you think I would ever make a deal with the devil's spawn without a backup plan?"

"You're an asshole," she shrilled.

"I've been called worse by a better class of people." I pressed the face of my watch against the security pad next to the elevator. "Come on, Tabitha. This is not my first rodeo. By the way, if you're recording our conversation right now, don't waste your fucking time. I have so much dirt on your shady dealings with Vargos that by the time I'm done snitching you out to the authorities, you'll end up in jail, designing uniforms for the entire prison."

"If you think this is done...well, you're sadly mistaken."

"It's done because I said it's done," I drawled while watching the green light flash quickly before the elevator door slid open. "Now slither back under the rock you came from." I hit the power button, and the call terminated before I marched onto the elevator, the door closing behind me.

One quick ride and the elevator door shifted open. I stepped out to find Zuri, my personal assistant. A curvy redhead, she was well dressed in a skintight cream dress, leaning against the wall while swiping her finger across the tablet in her other hand. She glanced up and smiled before pushing away from the wall and swaying toward me.

"Max," I voice-dialed.

I didn't break my step, and Zuri naturally kept pace as I strode farther into my soundproofed VIP lounge. It had been built to overlook Noire and provide me with the intimacy and comfort of a sanctuary away from the chaotic, sexually charged energy below.

"Hey, bro," Max answered.

"Anything interesting going on with Sin?"

Max, my friend and enforcer, had been staking out Sin's townhouse for days, and so far, there were no signs of anything. More importantly, there had been no male visitors.

"Nothing. What's up?"

"I just got a call from Tabitha, asking for more money. I need you to find her and shut her up. But don't kill her. I just want to make a statement that I can find her anytime, anyplace. Call me when it's done." Shoving my cell into my pocket, I marched over to my mahogany desk and sank into the leather chair tucked behind it.

"Calhoune just called. He's on his way," Zuri informed me.

"When he arrives, make him wait. I can't have him feeling too confident about our meeting."

Zuri handed over the tablet. "Here's Friday's guest list."

"When Bigsby shows, I want you to give him some of your smoldering Southern hospitality. Let's see how committed he is to his meal ticket, Cate Bellisario."

There was no doubt in my mind that Zuri would have Bigsby's dick harder than a rock with just one bat of her eyelashes. And when he took the bait, it would be more leverage that could be used to destroy him.

Men were enamored of Zuri's stunning beauty. She was feminine, delicate, and beguilingly innocent. Politicians, celebrities, businessmen—it didn't matter. All fell hard for her Lolita ways. That was what made her more than my assistant. She was an integral part of my team.

Zuri flipped her long, thick, red hair. "I'll make him feel real welcome, ya hear," she responded, switching seamlessly from her native New York accent to a deep Southern drawl.

I was constantly amazed by her gift for assuming cover identities. It was a skill she'd been taught at a young age to worm her way into the hearts of lonely men while her family of nomadic African travelers and thieves ruthlessly drained their victims' bank accounts.

"Good. Now take your Southern belle ass out of my sight. I have work to do." Effectively dismissing her, I scanned the guest list on the tablet.

I released a sigh when I didn't hear the click of her retreating heels, signaling her exit. I glanced up to find her staring at me with pursed lips.

I arched a brow. "Yes?"

Making herself comfortable in the chair in front of my desk, she let out a loud sigh and exclaimed, "These heels are killing me!"

"Zuri, that wasn't an invitation. I'm busy," I grumbled.

"Shit. Do you always have to be such a disgruntled ass?"

Sometimes I wished Zuri wasn't so open with her thoughts. I guessed years of friendship had given her that right.

I rubbed the side of my forehead where the throbbing had started. "I'm not fucking disgruntled. I'm working." My eyes narrowed. "Exactly what I'm paying you to do."

She smiled winningly. "Well, that's just plain rude. I do lots of work. It's not easy being the only ray of sunshine on a team of mean assholes."

Tilting my head to the ceiling, I let out a heavy sigh.

Zuri cleared her throat loudly.

I scrutinized her. "What do you want, Zuri?" Knowing her, she wouldn't shut up until she expressed her opinion.

She arched her brow. "You've been unusually distracted lately."

"What's your point?"

"I've been patient, but it's been weeks." She paused dramatically. "Are you ever going to mention the incident?"

I scowled at her. "What incident?"

"Rocco and Max told me about the 'rooftop incident'"—she made air quotes—"with Sin Michaels."

That was the other downside of working on a close-knit team. It was like a fucking high school. "Not that it's any of your damn business, but just for the record, there was no *incident*."

She blinked. "Sure there wasn't."

No matter how hard I glowered, as usual, she didn't seem a bit worried.

She smiled sweetly, too sweetly. "So the rumors were true."

"What rumors?"

"That you're about to fuck her like you're a recently released prisoner." She crossed her arms over her chest. "If it's true, that's a real bad idea."

"Go on." I was interested to see where her crazy line of logic would take her.

Uncrossing her arms, her eyes flashed angrily. "You're using her to get to Bigsby." She leaned forward. "This is wrong. You're mixing business with sex."

The reminder that I was breaking my number one rule of never mixing business with pleasure was fucking with my mind—big-time. My obsession with Sin was crazy and fucking reckless, but I found myself shaken by my need to possess her.

I shrugged. "I got this."

Zuri snorted. "You got this? Men. Can't live with them. Can't kill them," she spat, eyeballing me. "I've never seen you act like this over any other woman. You always catch and release. What makes her so different?"

To annoy her, I just stared at her.

"Well?" she asked, perturbed by the silence as she usually was.

I slid her a withering glare. "This is none of your business, Zuri."

Zuri gave me that tight smile of hers, the one that told me she was losing her patience. "I'm making it my business, because when she finds out she's been used like a whore, this is not going to end well—for you." She eyed me. "Believe me, hell hath no fury like a woman fucked over."

I smirked. "Oh, that's precious. You have a soft spot for Sin."

She blinked. "Give me a break with that bullshit. I just don't want your johnson getting in the way of business."

I'm Core McKay, a billionaire, and I'm always in control.

"Have I ever let a woman get in the way of business?" I grilled her.

"No. And that's what's got me worried about this Michaels chick. I know you. You want her. If you need to work off some of that sexual energy, let me arrange for Brenda to come out to Noire tomorrow night." She waggled her eyebrows. "She's been dying for you to play with her."

I blew out a noisy breath. Zuri knew me well, too well. I was a man with one simple vice—fucking. That was why I'd opened the McKay Club. It was my only indulgence, giving me unfettered access to beautiful women interested in uncommitted, hard-core sex. But lately, I'd been bored with all of them. My body and mind craved something different.

Sin...different.

"No. Brenda is too damn clingy." I ran my fingers through my hair in frustration. "I'm interested in playing with someone far more tempting." I rubbed my chin, wondering how Sin's dark tresses would look arranged against my pillow. My cock grew hard at the notion.

My thoughts were interrupted by Zuri's loud, animated voice.

"Oh God, you've already decided to fuck her." Zuri splayed her fingers out in a fan against her breastbone. "Whatever." She threw her hands up in the air. "I'm done trying to talk sense into you. I'll just sit back and watch the fireworks when she finds out you've manipulated her."

"If it happens, I'll deal with it." I wasn't worried about Sin finding out. Once I got her into my bed, she wouldn't be leaving until I was thoroughly sated.

Zuri inspected me with a small frown on her face, as though both disappointed in and surprised by me. "Yeah, okay. You keep telling yourself that, Core."

The tightness in my chest bore witness to the effect Zuri's words had on me, even though I wasn't ready to admit it, not even to myself.

❦ 2 ❦

SINTHIA

MY MUSCLES TIGHTENED in readiness as I slung my leather backpack over my shoulder. Then I locked my townhouse front door. Inhaling deeply through my nose and then exhaling through my mouth, I jogged down the steps toward Jade, who was leaning against her expensive red convertible.

"There she is, my marathon-running bestie," Jade greeted with a smirk on her face, pushing away from her car. Dramatically, she morphed her face into a mask of sheer terror as she jumped up and down while pointing down the block. "Oh, shit. Run, Sin. Run. I think I see Core coming this way. And look, he's swinging his big, bad cock." She threw her head back in a bray of laughter.

"Oh, shut the hell up, Jade." I stuck up my middle finger, trying to keep a straight face but failing. "It takes so little to amuse you." I chuckled.

It had been a couple weeks, but Jade hadn't let up on poking fun at me. Nope, not since I'd given her a synopsis of my embarrassing flight from Core after our rooftop foreplay session at Bigsby's charity gala.

"You said absolutely nothing about Core being little." Jade

wiggled her pinkie with an impish smile before pulling me in for a big hug.

I hugged her back hard, giving her a slight squeeze at the end before pulling away. "That's because he wasn't." I pinched her cheek playfully.

"Hot damn." Jade's apple-green eyes widened. "Was it wrist-wide?"

Turning away, I burst out in laughter. "All I'm saying is I swore an anaconda was pressing against my stomach." I grinned sassily before opening the passenger door and sliding in.

Jade laughed huskily. "You're a naughty girl," she stated before sauntering around to the driver's side.

"The naughtiest," I quipped as I slammed the door shut. Not wanting my hair to be whipped into a tangled bird's nest from the top-down convertible, I pulled it into a ponytail.

Jade got into the car, fastening her seat belt before turning the key and revving the engine. "Are you sure you want to do this?" she asked while pulling out of the parking space.

I sighed heavily, fastening my seat belt with angry, jerky movements. "You don't have to come, Jade. I can do this myself." That was something I'd repeated several times after I told her about our friend Francisco "Cisco" Rodriguez's call an hour ago.

He'd been practically giddy about the Manhattan gossip mill running rampant with breaking news that Tabitha, my former mentor and longtime friend, was back in town and frantically calling around, begging friends for money. Instantly, I'd dropped everything in my haste to go over to her house and confront her.

"Hell no!" Jade ripped her gaze away from the road long enough to give me the evil eye before turning back to concentrate on weaving through Manhattan traffic. "This is my chance to take part in a real-life, action-packed girl fight."

I shook my head. "You know this isn't some blockbuster movie, right?"

"No, it's going to be way better. I get to see you cunt-punt that backstabbing whore."

I mashed my lips together. "It makes me feel like shit that you're taking so much enjoyment in my Tabitha debacle." The debacle was that Tabitha had deliberately hidden the truth about the secret investor—aka Core McKay.

Jade jutted out her chin. "You mean it makes you feel like shit that she betrayed you, Sin." She reached one hand over and patted my leg in comfort. "Stop blaming yourself for something that wasn't your fault."

I tilted up my head, sighing dejectedly. "I should have known her brokered business deal was way too good to be true."

Good things never just happened to me. Shit, from the day I was born, I'd had to scratch and fight for every damn thing I wanted in life. So when Tabitha had called me out of the blue, all excited about one of her business connections willing to provide financing in exchange for a small percentage of my future profits, I was skeptical but desperate for funding to expand my business and start my new clothing line.

"So now you're kicking yourself for being ambitious?" Jade's tone was sharp.

I blew out a noisy breath. "No, I'm kicking myself for not asking questions."

I wanted to bang my head against the dashboard at how quickly I'd just blissfully signed the contract. The ink hadn't even dried on the business document when two million dollars were deposited into my business account with the promise of another million in six months. Little had I known that the investor was the one and only Core McKay or that I had stupidly given away ninety-seven percent of my business.

Frankly, that wasn't the part that hurt the most. It was that my trusted mentor and friend, Tabitha Thorp, had betrayed me by deliberately hiding the fact that my business investor was Core. My jaw tensed. Even worse, I had a damn sneaking suspicion that Tabitha and Core's relationship went deeper than business.

With disinterest, I glanced at the sleek concrete buildings as we raced over the Manhattan Bridge into Brooklyn.

But do I really want to know how deep?

Heat flushed through my body.

I took a cleansing breath. *It doesn't matter, not now.*

A bitter tang coated my mouth. What did matter was the fact that Tabitha had steered me into a deal that she knew I wouldn't have taken if I had known it involved Core. And given our long-standing friendship, in my eyes, that was a really fucked-up thing to do.

❦ 3 ❦

SINTHIA

JADE PULLED onto Tabitha's quiet residential block before parking in front of her brownstone. Jade drummed her fingers against the steering wheel. "So, what's the plan?"

"We wait to see if she's in there." My heart pounded as I eyed her home.

The normally vibrant flowers on the stairs were dead. Tabitha, if nothing else, was a stickler for order and appearances.

"Fuck it. I'm going in." Unbuckling my seat belt, I threw open the door.

Jade's eyes widened as she grabbed my arm. "Going in where?"

Shaking her off, I snapped, "Inside," before rushing out of the car.

Jade scrambled out, following me. "You're breaking in?" she squeaked, skirting around the car and jogging to catch up with me.

"No." I reached into my jeans pocket, pulling out a key. "I still have the spare key she gave me in case of an emergency while she was on vacation."

Her mouth slackened. "Sin, stop. This is fucking crazy."

I held up my hand. "I got this," I replied, scanning the neighborhood. I knew I wouldn't arouse any suspicion from the neighbors since, in the past, I'd been a frequent visitor to Tabitha's brownstone.

"I'm not letting you go in by yourself."

I whirled around to face her and whispered, "You can't come in with me. I need you out here, keeping watch, just in case shit goes south. So keep your finger on your cell and get ready to call your family's well-paid attorney, because I, for damn sure, don't want to end up in jail as Big Bertha's bitch."

Jade ran a jerky hand through her hair. "Okay, but I'm giving you fifteen minutes. If you're not back, I'm coming in."

"Deal," I muttered before turning on my heel and sprinting up the stairs.

Bouncing on my toes, I stuck the key into the lock and entered Tabitha's house. Holding my breath, I punched the code on the alarm, hoping Tabitha hadn't changed it. The alarm deactivated, and I sagged against the wall with relief. The pounding of my heart slowed down.

"Thank God," I mumbled, shoving the key back into my pocket.

I nearly swallowed my tongue when I finally got my shit together enough to scan her house.

The space was completely cleared out.

"What the hell?" I murmured with a heavy feeling in my stomach.

My heartbeat raced as I rushed around the empty house. "What in the world is going on?" I jogged upstairs. It was empty too. "I can't believe this." I felt a fluttering in my belly as I ran back downstairs.

There was nothing to see here. I secured the alarm and door before stomping down the stairs.

A flood of adrenaline still tingled through my body as I slid into the convertible.

Jade's eyebrows furrowed and then released. "So, no Tabitha?"

"Nope. She cleaned out her house. It's as if she never existed."

"Shit." Jade peeled away. Then she drove onto Flatbush Avenue, racing toward the Manhattan Bridge. "I don't get it."

I threw up my hands. "Welcome to my world."

I really didn't understand what was going on. The whole ride back from Brooklyn into Manhattan was a blur of chaotic questions. *Where is Tabitha? Why did she abruptly pull up roots? Is she dead?*

It seemed Jade's mind was also racing. Suddenly, she murmured, "This shit is crazy as hell, even for dragon lady Tabitha."

I arched a brow. "You think? Just a couple weeks ago, we were at the McKay Club, laughing and drinking. Now her brownstone is cleared out, with no trace of her." I undid my ponytail and shook out my hair. "I need a drink." Slipping off my sneakers, I pulled my stilettos from my designer leather backpack before putting them on.

"I second that. Our favorite place?"

"You know it." I swiped on lip gloss while staring out at the New York City night traffic as we whizzed through the city.

It didn't take long for us to arrive at our favorite Tribeca dinner place. Jade relinquished the convertible to the overeager valet. We took a few quick steps toward the inconspicuous doorman, who opened the creepy-looking black door, allowing Jade and me to step into the trendy speakeasy.

At the entrance, the willowy hostess with large breasts on display approached us with a huge smile. "Hello, ladies. Welcome back. Please come this way." Using her high-pitched voice, she directed us to follow.

Jade and I were escorted through a private entrance into the retro-styled, closet-sized monochrome space. It was bat cave-level murky, barely letting us see the waiters and waitresses, but that was the point. It wasn't a place to be seen or to see.

We paraded past the banquettes and small tables in the Lshaped portion of the room and private booths, and we went right up to the dark and narrow bar. It possessed the same caliber and quality that came with a five-star restaurant, without the fussiness of a dining room. We loved hanging out at the bar and eating small portions we could share, making it more of a communal meal with a casual vibe. Besides, it was the best seat in the house because it was within arm's reach of the bartender.

Settling down, I was determined to make the best of the evening, and I focused on enjoying a well-deserved girls' night out.

Jade's eyes widened with interest when a lanky bartender with floppy curls and a disarming smile edged close to us. "Well, look what we have here," Jade remarked while sinking down onto a chair. "A new bartender."

He beamed at us. "Ladies, how may I serve you?"

"Let me see..." Jade twirled her jet-black hair, smiling coyly at him. "How about—"

I elbowed her in the side, hard. "Really?"

"What?" Her eyes widened playfully. "He asked, and I have needs. Lots of wicked, dirty needs." She displayed a wide grin.

I rolled my eyes heavenward before glancing at the red-faced but interested bartender. "Two shots of vodka," I responded.

He chuckled before roaming away, and he returned minutes later with two small silver cups, placing them before us. "You two look like you're up to trouble tonight. What's the celebration?" he inquired.

I nodded toward Jade. "Troublemaker is off to New Zealand on a movie shoot."

"Wow. Congrats." He blinked rapidly and then stared openly at Jade. "What would you lovely ladies like for your next round?"

There were no cocktail menus. It was a simple process. We'd let the bartender know what type of alcohol and flavors we longed for, and then he would return with his creations.

Jade's tongue darted out to touch her lips. "Surprise us," she drawled.

He got a little flustered, not unusual for most men in Jade's presence. "Got it," he stammered before plodding away.

"To Team Us," we toasted before smelling the vodka while swirling it in our glasses.

Taking a small sip, I let the flavor rest on my palate for a few seconds before swallowing it, savoring the aftertaste.

"Why do you like them so young?" I needled.

"Because they're so pliable," Jade moaned. "And eager to learn."

"You mean, you like the control." It was a statement, not a question.

Jade snorted. "Like you don't. Knowing you, you orchestrate every move in bed." She mimicked my voice as she said, "Move your mouth here. Um...no, no, no. More tongue, less teeth. Wait. Are you done already?"

I choked out a laugh because she was spot-on. "I can't help it that I have high expectations no man has yet to live up to."

"Uh-huh. Says the woman who hasn't been fucked in months. Shit. You just gave up trying."

"I'll have you know I had mind-numbing, toe-curling sex with Beast last night." I left out the part that the toe-curling was courtesy of dirty thoughts of Core going down on me.

I shivered deliciously. *Jesus, I bet his tongue game is absolutely spectacular.*

"Beast is your vibrator. It doesn't count," Jade interjected.

"Hells yeah, it does. Beast is way better than any man." I ticked off my points. "He follows directions. He stays hard for hours. And he doesn't bitch and moan or beg to stay when I kick him the fuck out of my bed."

Jade groaned. "I'm going to have to get you laid fast before you decide to marry Beast."

A waiter with a handlebar mustache drifted over to us with menus. "Hello, ladies. The same? Or would you like to try something new?"

"The same," we agreed in unison.

The waiter retreated. We watched with fascination as the pretty-boy bartender worked. He was like a mad scientist of booze.

I nudged her with my elbow. "So, are you excited about your trip?"

I was elated yet sad that Jade was flying out to New Zealand tomorrow morning to begin production on her first directorial feature. She was going to be away on the shoot for months, and I was going to miss her something fierce.

"More like scared," Jade confessed with a hint of a smile. "I can't believe I'm about to step behind the camera with my own script. It was fun just blithely writing whatever I wished without having to worry about whether the movie studios would buy my script. Now I'm terrified about the reality of production. The success or failure of my movie is all on me."

I rubbed her hand comfortingly. "I read your script, and it's really good. You'll make it work."

Jade smiled. "And that's why I love you so much. You believe in me without a doubt."

I grinned at her. "That's how besties roll."

The waiter came back with small sharing plates of beef tenderloin skewers with chimichurri salsa, truffle mac and cheese, parmesan truffle fries, and a trio of bar snacks. We dug in hungrily. The bartender reappeared with our drinks, set them down, and jaunted away. I sipped the drink that tasted of several delicious flavors—rum, lemon, maple syrup, and hellfire bitters.

"Sin." Jade twirled her glass. "Why don't you come to New Zealand with me? Get away for a little bit since your collection is almost completed." She smiled cheekily. "Meet yourself a man. You know what they say. What happens in New Zealand stays in New Zealand."

I choked on my drink. "What happens in New Zealand stays in New Zealand?"

"That's what I heard," she boasted.

I snorted. "First, fucking no one says that shit...like ever.

Second, I can't relax until my collection is done." I worriedly bit my bottom lip, contemplating the reality that I might never be able to relax.

"You mean, you won't. There's a big difference," Jade stated. "Sin, things between you and Core are fabulous. Stop looking for a fire where there isn't one."

I sighed heavily. Maybe Jade was right. I should be ecstatic about the fact that, due to Core's arm-twisting, I had received confirmation from all retailers that they were back on board with carrying my collection. Now I was working around the clock to complete my pieces, and Core was handling all the business and financial matters. It was a perfect partnership—maybe too perfect.

With an elbow on the bar, Jade rested her chin on her palm and fixed her eyes on me. "So what really happened between you and Core at the gala? And I want details."

It had been such a busy couple of weeks, with Jade wrapping up shooting for her television show and me frantically trying to finish my collection, that we hadn't managed much communication, except for brief calls and texts.

"Hmm?" I asked before popping a forkful of mac and cheese into my mouth.

"Don't *hmm* me. Why did you run from Core?"

"He scared the shit out of me," I confessed. "No other man has ever made me feel so utterly consumed and possessed."

It was ridiculous how much I'd let my hot foreplay session with Core rattle me. The way his lips had devoured mine, the roughness of his callused fingers against my skin, and the overwhelming urge to fall to my knees, begging him to take me in any position he saw fit, had spurred a surprising fight-or-flight response.

I'd chosen flight, which was terrifying and humiliating.

When I'd weaved my way back into the gala, my palms had been sweaty and my heart had been beating so fast I seriously had thought I was one step away from having a heart attack. Not wanting to spend another minute at the gala, I'd faked a migraine and told Jade I needed to leave early. Thankfully, Kirby, Jade's chauffeur had dropped me at home, leaving Jade to ride home with her mother. And later that night, I'd crawled into bed with Core's name on my lips and my fingers playing with my womanhood.

"I'm going to need a lot more slutty details," Jade demanded in a singsong voice.

"Okay." I covered my eyes. "I almost hiked up my gown and fucked him right there on the rooftop." I peeked through my fingers. "I'm a slut, right?"

Jade blinked twice, hard. "Uh...no."

I frowned at her. "There was hesitation in your response."

Her eyes were filled with laughter. "Because I just don't get it. If you want to have sex with him, go ahead and do it. You're a sensual woman. He's a smoking-hot billionaire. You're both obviously attracted to each other. Just fuck him and walk away." She shrugged. "No biggie."

If only it were that simple...

The memory of his touch, taste, and voice was already imprinted on my body and mind. Just the thought of the emotional damage he could inflict once I let him into my body made my mouth taste like sawdust.

The smiling waiter meandered up to us.

"So? Are you going to fuck him or not?" Jade demanded.

The waiter swallowed hard, watching us with wide eyes. "Anything else?" he croaked.

"No, we're good," I replied unblinkingly.

He hurried away like he couldn't move fast enough.

I turned to Jade. "No, I'm not going to have sex with Core."

"Uh-huh," Jade responded before taking a sip of her drink, peering at me over the rim.

I pursed my lips. "Don't stare at me like that."

"You're lying to yourself. I saw how you were eye-banging Core at the gala."

"I want him. That's a fact." I sighed. "But business and hot sex don't mix."

"Since when?"

My mind yelled, *Since Core!*

Taking a sip of my drink, I remained silent.

Jade continued, undeterred. "What would it hurt if you just saw where this thing with him might go?"

I shook my head. "Given my bad luck with men, it will be disastrous." *Both emotionally and financially.*

"Such a drama queen." Jade rolled her eyes heavenward. "Admit it. You're scared of getting hooked on his hot ass."

The truth of her words made my stomach plummet.

I twirled my glass. "What happens if I do and things get really weird with our business relationship?"

Jade raised her eyebrow. "Cross that bridge when you get there. Are you going to have sex with him?"

"Yes," slipped out. "I mean no," I snapped. But my sex-deprived body yelled, *Hells yes!*

"Yes?" Jade pursed her lips. "No?" She pulled on a strand of my hair. "Which is it?"

I scowled at her defiantly. "It's complicated."

I drained what was left in my glass before motioning the bartender over. I didn't even have to ask. He already had two drinks in his hands. He expertly removed the empty glasses before pushing fresh drinks within our fingertips' reach. I took a sip. It was a gin gimlet with just the right amount of tart and tangy. It was quite refreshing and delicious.

Jade regarded me, wide-eyed, over her glass. "Hmm...complicated. So what you're really saying is if you'd met him under different circumstances, you would?" She popped another appetizer into her mouth while examining me like a specimen under a microscope.

My eye twitched. "Why are we even talking about this?" I grabbed another appetizer.

She leaned closer. "Why are you getting so agitated?"

My eyes narrowed. "I didn't intend for any of this shit to happen. I had a pretty damn good plan." I always lived my life by well-conceived plans. It kept things…well, orderly. "Take the money from the secret investor, complete my collection, get it into the retailers, work that bad boy until I made a profit, and give the investor back the money." I chewed my bottom lip. "Now I feel totally stuck, because without him and his money, my collection will never see the light of day." I didn't have to add that my obligation to Core had been adding up, sending me further and further into his debt.

Core was the spider, and I was the fly caught in his web. My gut twisted—and not in the I'm-scared way. It was more like the I'm-fucking-turned-on way. That was how sick and demented I was.

Jade squealed dramatically. "Oh shit! Your eyes just dilated." She pointed at me. "Admit it. His bad-boy swagger has your lady bits all in a quiver."

My lips pressed together in a slight grimace. "I'm not confirming or denying."

We both knew I loved bad boys, and I had a habit of attracting and collecting them like Ken dolls. It was a gift and a curse. Thus far, the mysterious and eccentric Core McKay was the baddest boy I'd encountered. Yet there was so much I didn't really know about him, except for what the gossip hags whispered about—that he'd built his billion-dollar empire through drug trafficking, money laundering, and prostitution, and that was only to mention a few of the criminally speculated trades.

Jade started loudly humming the "Bad Boys" song.

"I'm not doing another bad boy ever." I took a large gulp of my drink. "Remember Kyle?"

Jade narrowed her eyes into slits. "Are you kidding me? Core and Kyle seem nothing alike. Core is alpha-delicious. Kyle is a cheating prick." Her eyes softened. "Sin, you've got to get over Kyle."

My brows came together in a puzzled frown. "I have."

Jade stared.

"It's true. Seeing Kyle again at Bigsby's gala was not the heart-stopping train wreck I'd dreaded for years. I felt absolutely nothing—no pitter-patter of my heart, no I-wish-he-were-mine-again angst. Shit, I said a silent thankful prayer to the universe that the conceited, egotistical douchebag was someone else's problem."

"All of that might be true, but every man you've met after him has paid the price for the Kyle clusterfuck."

She was right. For so many years, I had allowed my bitter past with Kyle to steal my chances for a normal relationship with every single guy I met after him.

"That's the truth. But what's even more pathetic is that Kyle was never even worth the heartache." I shrugged. "But I was young and naïve. Catching him cheating in such a fucked-up manner tainted my notion of trust and relationships." I cringed just thinking about the night of happiness that had turned into dust the minute I pushed open his bedroom door.

Kyle stood with his designer jeans gathered around his ankles while his cock was being fondled by some chick with perfectly smooth, highlighted blond hair that fell across her shoulders like a gorgeous curtain.

I froze, shocked, with my mouth gaping open, as if it were some sort of mirage. I watched as the chick glided up with too much sway in her narrow hips. Then she gave me a smug look before sauntering out of the bedroom, and it felt like a dagger to the heart.

"Kyle? How could you do this to me?" I rasped, unchecked tears streaming down my cheeks. "I love you." My voice hitched.

His face turned into a mask of hate that shocked me to my very core. "Love?" He huffed out an arctic laugh. "Sin, this isn't love. It never was, and it never will be."

I flinched like a punch had been launched to my gut. "If this isn't love, then tell me, what the hell is it?" I stared at him with narrowed eyes, feeling my heart ice over inch by inch.

"What do you want from me? I haven't promised you anything, Sin," he sneered while unhurriedly buckling his belt.

"We've been dating for months!" I yelled.

His jaw tightened. "No, we've been fucking for months." He walked up and stared at me without a trace of emotion in his beautiful blue eyes. "Sin, I'm going away to college, and you're staying here to work for your mother. It would never work out between us."

He reached out to touch my hair, but I smacked his hand away.

He shrugged. "Take it for what it was. We're over."

I stood there feeling stupid that I'd allowed myself to be weakened after my dad's death. I couldn't believe I'd let Kyle into my heart and body. I never would have let him in if I had known he would hurt me and leave me drowning in the deep end.

"Over?" I froze like a deer in headlights.

Gasping for breath, I sank into the murky waters of an emotional abyss.

Then he went for the ultimate emotional bitch slap. "Let's keep it real, Sin. What we had was fun but temporary. You and I know there's no way in hell I could bring you home to my parents. You just don't fit into my world." His parting words burned, fueling my hate fire.

Jade nudged me, interrupting my disturbing trip down memory lane. "Sin, I'm not saying to forget. I'm saying you need to heal and let that shit go."

"Let it go? I've done that, but the healing part takes a willingness to open up my heart to a man who's worthy. I've met men who are losers, liars, users, and looking for another heart to break, but I haven't met anyone worthy." I pursed my lips. "But that's the story of my fucked-up life. Always finding Mr. Wrong."

"I refuse to give up just because we've both kissed more than our share of frogs. That shit doesn't mean Mr. Love Me Right isn't out there."

I looked at her like she'd lost her damn mind. "Are you kidding me?"

Jade regarded me with a pained expression before waving over the pretty-boy bartender. "We're going to need more drinks over here."

Already anticipating our need, he brought over two more drinks, and then he moseyed away. Jade sat up, peering over the bar.

I snapped my fingers in her face. "Will you take your eyes off his ass?" I admonished, even though it really was an awe-inspiring butt.

As if sensing Jade's heated stare, he grinned over his shoulder at her.

Jade bit her lower lip. "Damn. He's yummy but absolutely not 'the one.'" She made air quotes. "I've done more guys like him than I care to count. Gorgeous but dullsville in bed."

I raised my glass in a mock salute. "Cheers to the few women in Manhattan who are crazy enough to take one for Team Single and Desperately Seeking a Good Fuck."

Jade choked with laughter. "Finding a halfway decent man to fuck is like wading through a cesspool. It's disgusting and leaves you smelling like shit."

I gave her a playful nudge. "Exactly."

To prove my point about the bleakness of the dating game, I quickly scanned the space. "Okay, prime example over there."

I nodded in the direction of a table with flickering candle-light and a beautiful blond woman who was staring blankly at her date—a hot-looking guy with an artfully messy fauxhawk, probably thanks to gallons of hair gel. He was boasting loudly about rubbing elbows with celebrities, business moguls, and politicians during his recent trip to St. Thomas on his newly purchased yacht.

"See her blank-faced stare? I bet she's contemplating which fake orgasm moan, high-pitched or low and throaty, she'll use while he's fucking her tonight."

I nodded over to the end of the bar at the middle-aged man dressed like he'd just stepped off the red carpet for the teen awards. He draped his arm around a busty young brunette. Then he winked at me while licking the rim of his glass in an icky, sexually suggestive manner. "And Mr. Midlife Crisis over there is having some delusional fantasy about a threesome with me and that brunette pasted to his side." I shuddered with distaste. "Hard pass on that shit."

Jade smacked the bar. "True that. The problem is men are clueless about what women really want—foreplay and oral sex."

I snorted. "Hence, the problem. Men wouldn't know how to go down on a woman even if she wrote step-by-step instructions, taped them to her cunt, and shone a flashlight on them."

Jade chuckled. "Exactly. That's why I've been doing some serious thinking."

Uh-oh. Not good.

She continued. "Don't you ever wonder about what's next in your life?"

"Are you fucking with me right now? Or are you running your lines for your movie?" I popped another appetizer into my mouth, chewing happily.

"Neither." She shrugged. "Ever since my mom started getting serious with that lawyer Erika hooked her up with—"

I choked on a mouthful of food. "They're serious?"

Ariana Bellisario, Jade's mother, was worse than both of us when it came to men. After her nasty divorce, she'd kept men at a distance, but that wouldn't stop her from taking an occasional lover when it suited her.

"Yep, very."

My mouth fell open. "Wow!"

"If she can change, maybe there's still hope for us."

There was a hardening in my stomach. "I doubt it."

Jade's mouth twisted into a grimace. "Have you ever thought about where we would be today if we weren't so emotionally fucked up?"

The bartender lingered while removing our glasses and presenting two fresh drinks.

Pointedly, I eyed him, urging him to keep it moving. He grinned sheepishly.

Turning my head back to Jade, I replied, "Excuse me? I'm not emotionally fucked up. You are."

She snorted. "Okay, so now you're delusional. Our idea of a perfect date is fucking a guy until we pass out and then kicking him out before daylight."

The bartender choked.

Jade winked at him coyly. "Interested?"

His pupils dilated. "Sounds like a match made in heaven," he responded before striding away.

I glowered at his retreating back and then looked back at Jade. "All confirming my original assessment. You're the one who's emotionally challenged, not me."

"I'm about to turn twenty-seven." She looked off into the distance for a moment, and then she scrutinized me. "And I think it's time for a change."

I propped my elbow on the bar, placing my chin into my palm. "I've only known one good man in my entire life, and that was my dad. He was way more man than Grace deserved."

"Your mother is a nutjob." Jade curled her upper lip in disdain. "And my sperm donor screwed me over big time. Now, every time I meet a guy, I can't help questioning whether he wants me for my fame, money, family name, or all of it. That's a really fucked-up way to think."

I took a sip of my drink. "Really, I'm good with my life, Jade. I have a best friend who's like my sister, Ariana, who's the mother that I never had, a beautiful home, and a successful career. I'm damn happy."

Jade tilted her head to the side. "Are you?"

I put down my drink. "Am I what?"

"Happy?"

I formed my fingers into a steeple, considering the question. "Yes." I scowled at my almost empty glass and then gazed over at her. "Have I thought about what it would be like to roll over and bump into a warm body instead of a cold, empty bed? The thought has crossed my mind." I left out the word *lately*. "But honestly, I don't think I'm built for that level of commitment."

Jade sighed. "I think that's what we've been telling ourselves for so long that we actually believe it. This much I know. Someday, I want kids and stability. Don't you want children one day?"

My mouth went dry. "No," I answered firmly. "I don't trust myself not to turn into a monster, cruel and unloving, like Grace. I would never do that to a child."

My life growing up had been an emotional roller coaster, all due to my mother, Grace. Dad had done the best he could to shield me from her verbal and emotional abuse, but still, it just hadn't been enough.

"Grace is a bitch. You're nothing like her."

"I hope not." My pulse sped up. "She never loved me or my dad, and it changed us for the worse. We both morphed into people who lived just to please her—hoping if we changed, if we could be everything she wanted, she would love us. It took me years to learn loving myself was good enough. I don't need a man to validate me—not now, not ever."

"Fuck validation. I'm talking about having the right man to love you for who you are. A partnership of equals."

I let out a sigh of despair. "There's no damn happily ever after when it comes to men and relationships. That's a fairy tale. Reality is way bleaker and darker." I nudged her playfully. "Now, enough of this serious stuff. Tonight is about having fun and celebrating. I think a call to Kirby is in order, because we're about to get fucked up tonight."

Jade swiped her finger across her cell, tapped out a text, and shoved it into her bag. "Done. Our chariot will be waiting outside when we roll out, all liquored up." She winked at the bartender, her index finger gesturing for him to bring his fine ass over. "Keep them coming, baby, because we can go all night."

With an open gaze, he met Jade's eyes directly. "So can I," he responded.

"Really?" Jade asked, licking her lips.

"Yep." He winked at her before roaming away.

"Holy shit." Jade fanned herself. "I think there's movement in my vajayjay, an honest-to-goodness tingly sensation."

I sputtered, "Are you sure that's not the aftereffect from the Brazilian wax job you got today?"

Jade slapped my arm.

I laughed. "Please don't fuck him. I actually love this place and his drinks. If you have sex with him, he'll get all mad and pouty when he realizes it's a one-time bang extravaganza."

Jade shooed me. "He's a big boy." She waggled her eyebrows. "Hopefully, a very big boy."

I shook my head with fake dismay. "And this conversation is officially over."

❦ 4 ❦

CORE

BIGSBY SAUNTERED across my expansive VIP lounge with a determined swagger. His confidence quickly dissipated as I deliberately said nothing, letting the cooling sound of silence speak volumes.

He stood before my desk and nodded at Ram, my business partner, then at Rocco, my enforcer who handled all my dirty work along with his brother, Max. Both were my family, closer than flesh and blood. I'd take a bullet for any one of them, and I knew they'd do the same for me.

Standing to my left, Rocco crossed his arms and widened his stance. And to my right, Ram stared at Bigsby with a pinched face until Bigsby broke eye contact first by glancing away.

Bigsby cleared his throat before offering his hand to me. "Hello, McKay."

I ignored his outstretched hand as my expression darkened at the unmistakable glint of diamonds and rubies on Bigsby's middle finger. It was like a bullet through the heart. This man standing before me was a cold-blooded killer...who had murdered my mother. Rage surged through my body like a dark, violent thunderstorm, and all the bitter memories came flooding back.

My heart leaped out of my chest when my mother screamed, "Leave my son alone, you fucking asshole. This is between you and me, you damn coward."

The man pulled a .357 Magnum from his beltline. "Shut the fuck up, whore. You brought this on yourself. I warned you to keep your damn mouth shut!" he yelled while grabbing her by the hair with one hand.

Turning her face away from him, the man placed the gun to her head. It seemed like an eternity to me as I memorized the gold ruby-and-diamond-encrusted horseshoe ring on his middle finger.

"McKay?" Bigsby's voice pierced through the recollection of my mother's death.

My lips flattened.

Bigsby's smug-cat smile slipped before he dropped his hand.

Tilting my head, I still had my gaze fixed on his ring. "As I mentioned at your political fundraising event a couple weeks ago, I still cannot get over how unique that ring is. Where did you get it?"

Bigsby smiled cockily, letting himself settle into the chair directly in front of my desk with exaggerated casualness. "I had it made in the eighties. There's only one of its kind."

My face was a cold mask, hiding my bitter hatred. "Interesting."

I studied him for a few minutes. Bigsby shifted nervously, his hands clamped over the armrests of the chair.

Bigsby's smile seemed forced. "Thank you for accepting my request to meet, McKay."

"How can I help you, Calhoune?"

Bigsby's facial muscles twitched before he shook his head in dismay. "Damn, the rumors are true. You really like to get straight down to business."

"Because everyone knows it's all I give a shit about."

"Well, that's great." Bigsby sat forward. "Because I have a big moneymaking venture you'll love."

I gave a halfhearted shrug. "There's nothing you can offer me that I don't already have, Bigsby."

Bigsby crossed and uncrossed his leg. "How about the Port District?"

"I'm listening," I replied in a sharp tone.

His jaw tightened. "As you know, I'll be New York City's next mayor."

"That statement is highly debatable, but continue," I muttered.

"When I'm mayor"—anger flashed across Bigsby's eyes—"I will own the city, including the port."

Shit just got very interesting. The Port District of New York and New Jersey encompassed part of seventeen counties in the region.

"Keep going," I ordered tonelessly.

Bigsby's posture stiffened. "I need your overseas connections for a little matter on my end." He cleared his throat loudly. "I understand from my sources that you're a minor stakeholder in Sin Michaels Corporation."

I chuckled darkly. Bigsby was fishing for information. He'd have to work fucking harder to get anything from me.

"Minor? I own the business. And her," I replied calmly. "Cut to the chase, Calhoune. What do you want?"

Bigsby's body tightened as he ran his hand over his salt-and-pepper hair with agitation. "I've also been informed you're set to manufacture in Thailand, and your first run to the United States will be in weeks."

"And?" I inclined my head for him to continue.

Bigsby cleared his throat. "I just need a small area within your cargo shipment to put my merchandise. If you agree, I'll ensure there are no issues at the port when your shipment arrives."

"I see. So, if I don't agree, you'll make it complicated and expensive to get my merchandise into New York?" The final words were furious and guttural.

The chunky gold ruby-and-diamond-encrusted horseshoe

ring on Bigsby's middle finger glinted as he nervously adjusted his cuff. "That could be a real possibility."

Glancing up from his ring, I asked, "What type of merchandise?"

"Does it matter?" He pressed his lips together.

My nostrils flared. "I'm not going to blindly ship merchandise without knowing exactly what it is, especially if it's illegal."

"My informants tell me you don't have issues with getting your hands dirty." He cleared his throat and leaned forward in emphasis. "That's why I'm coming to you with this sensitive matter."

"Sensitive matter? I guess that's code for pimping out girls to your rich friends," I stated matter-of-factly.

Bigsby's mouth hung open. "How did you—" He sputtered over the words.

I cut him off. "My connections love to talk." I left out the fact that the majority of my information came from a now-dead Ben Vargos. "Especially when they're paying a shitload of money to fuck pretty college girls in any way and anywhere they want." I paused for a moment. "Let's cut to the chase, shall we? I know you're running women," I stated bluntly. "I don't deal in sex trafficking. So my response to your business offer is fuck no."

The vein along Bigsby's jaw pulsed rapidly. "I'll give you a thirty-percent cut. That's a deal worth five hundred million dollars."

"I'm accepting all the risk. I want a fifty-fifty split." I scrutinized Bigsby, assessing his level of desperation.

He gawked at me, speechless, before breaking eye contact and then glaring at me. "Deal."

I smirked. He was desperate to accept my throat-cutting deal.

Bigsby stood up, fidgeting. "Will there be an issue with Ms. Michaels?"

"As I told you, I own both the company and her," I stated without any emotion.

Bigsby smiled, but it didn't quite reach his eyes. "Excellent. We'll be talking, McKay," he added before marching out.

I waited for the elevator ding, the signal that Bigsby was gone. "I should have known what that piece of shit was up to." I slapped my palm down on the desk with a resounding noise.

Now Bigsby's interest in Sin's business made more sense. No one would ever suspect a naïve designer would be part of a sex-trafficking ring. Frankly, Bigsby's plan was brilliant.

Ram trudged over to the bar. He poured a drink, a very strong one, and gulped it. "I seriously wanted to rip out his windpipe. That unscrupulous fuck is hiding Jeff's location." He squeezed the glass in his hand. "I swear, if Jeff killed my sister, I'll..." His eyes took on a steely glint.

Ram had been blaming himself for her disappearance, for not stepping in when Lexis had gushed about the perfect guy she'd met at a party near campus. The guy, Jeff Barolo, had become Lexis's boyfriend after dating her for only two weeks.

I tightened my fists. "Don't even fucking think it."

It was hard as hell to watch my level-headed friend slowly becoming emotionally unhinged. We both knew the odds of Lexis being alive were slim, but I was still optimistic. It didn't matter that Lexis had made a lot of fucked-up decisions—dropping out of college and running away with Jeff. She didn't deserve to die.

I strode from my leather chair to the bar, pouring myself a scotch. "We're getting closer to finding Lexis—alive."

Rocco chimed in with his brows knitted. "The sooner we find her, the better, bro."

Kevin, my tech genius, burst into the room. "Listen to this. Bigsby just made a call," he exclaimed excitedly, holding his laptop in one hand.

Ram's eyes grew wide. "How the hell did you record it so fast?"

Kevin's forehead creased into a frown. "I set up a fake cell phone tower, allowing me to spy on him," he stated nonchalantly.

Rocco's stoic expression turned grim. "We're all going to fucking jail."

Kevin squinted. "Only idiots get caught."

"Will you two just shut the hell up?" I snapped. "Kevin, play it."

Kevin pressed a key on his laptop.

Bigsby's voice began. "Jeff, good news. I just made a deal with that bastard McKay."

"Good. I'm tired of clients whining about needing new girls," Jeff remarked.

"I'll make arrangements to move the goods, but there's only one loose end. I need you to break in to Sin's house by tomorrow night and find that damn ledger. It's the only leverage I still have on this city," Bigsby finished.

"No problem. But what do you want me to do about Sin if she's home?" Jeff asked.

"If she gets in the way, rough her up a little, but don't kill her. I still need her alive," Bigsby warned before disconnecting.

What the hell? Rough her up? Oh, fuck no.

I eyed Kevin. "I need answers now. What's the connection between Sin and Bigsby?"

"I'm waiting for my informant to get back to me," Kevin replied.

"You've been working on getting information for days. What's the fucking holdup?" I mashed my lips together. "Call your connection. Triple the amount of money for a solid lead."

Kevin's mouth gaped open. "Shit. Triple?"

"Do it," I responded in a deadly voice.

Kevin pulled out his cell and tapped it. "I need that info I requested *now*," he demanded to the person on the phone. "No more time. I don't give a shit what you're working on." He peered at me, holding up four fingers.

His greedy informant was asking for quadruple the standard rate. I nodded in agreement.

"You got it," Kevin told the informant. "Now get me the fucking info." He paced back and forth with his cell pressed against his ear. "Like I give a shit what you're in the middle of. Move it."

Pinching the bridge of my nose, I waited while Kevin continued to gather intel.

Kevin's face stilled. "Holy shit! Are you sure?" He frowned. "Okay. Yes." He paused. "Yes, I got it. But I want you to keep working that angle." He knitted his brows, his bewilderment evident, as he shoved his cell into his pocket.

I crossed my arms, looking at Kevin as he plopped down on the edge of the desk.

"So?"

Kevin raked a hand over his face. "In the eighties, Bigsby ran a prostitution ring out of his strip joint."

I glared at him. "That's it?"

Kevin held up his hand. "I'm not finished."

"That's a relief, because your intel is straight-up garbage," Ram muttered.

Kevin shot him a nasty glare. "Anyway, this is where things get interesting. Bigsby started rolling with some powerful NYC players. I'm talking about politicians, judges, and Wall Street executives."

"That doesn't make sense." Rocco interrupted. "There's no way in hell a thug like Bigsby could get in good with rich guys."

"He could if he was supplying them with girls for sex," I rebutted.

As the son of a stripper, I'd learned fast about the underbelly of strip clubs. Bitterness filled my mouth as I thought about the nights when Mom would bring me into work because she was too broke to pay for a babysitter. My nose wrinkled with distaste as the faces of the women she'd worked with flashed through my head—young, reeking of alcohol, junkies with eyes glazed over.

I'd caught them on their knees, giving blow jobs to customers in dark corners or hallways.

"That's exactly what Bigsby was doing, and he was raking in tons of money. Then, for some unknown reason, he and his business partner went their separate ways." Kevin regarded me smugly. "Guess who his partner was?"

"Sin's father," I snapped.

Ram arched a brow. "Which one?"

I sighed heavily.

Kevin's previous investigation into Sin's family background unearthed that she had two birth certificates, each one showing a different set of parents. The first birth certificate had her father listed as Ian Michaels and her mother as Grace Michaels. The second certificate had her father listed as Greer Lorne Cruickshank and her mother as Aubrey Cruickshank.

"Greer Lorne Cruickshank," Kevin replied. "After Greer and Bigsby dissolved their business partnership, Greer was found dead in an apartment fire."

I bunched my shoulders, but I kept my face expressionless. "Cruickshank?" I bit back the expletive hovering on my tongue.

What the hell?

Cruickshank was the person Bigsby had bragged about to Mom before killing her.

Ram's brows drew together. "What are the circumstances of the fire?"

"Arson," Kevin replied flatly. "Bigsby mysteriously disappeared after that."

I stiffened my shoulders. "Now he's back, and the fucker reinvented himself."

Rocco scratched his chin. "I don't get it. Why would Bigsby run for mayor and risk his past being dredged up? That's political suicide."

"What past?" Kevin's brows furrowed. "Do you know how hard it was for me just to get this much information on him?" He shook his head. "It took a shitload of money and power to clean his record. Now, he looks like some fucking altar boy."

"And he seems untouchable." I tapped my fingers against the desk while contemplating the situation. "The ledger must be the only evidence linking him to his former life."

Knowing what I knew so far about Bigsby, I knew he had come too far to let his new life disintegrate, which meant Sin's safety was in serious jeopardy if she had the ledger.

"I want that damn ledger," I hissed before glancing over at Rocco. "You and Max stake out Sin's house. No need for us to get our hands dirty on this one. Just wait for that idiot Jeff to break in and find the ledger. Snatch him when you see it in his hand."

Ram inclined his head toward me. "And what are you going to do about Sin?"

My face hardened, and I drew up to my full, intimidating height. "Let me worry about that."

❦ *5* ❦

SINTHIA

After sculpting and draping the fabric directly onto the mannequin, I stepped back with a critical eye. "Not bad," I mumbled under my breath.

Normally, I'd sculpt directly onto my body while sitting in front of a mirror and ask my intern, Giselle, to take a picture of me to capture the shape when it was pinned to me. Draping was almost as good but a tad bit slower.

Turning around, I threw a stray piece of fabric into a wooden box with rattan trim. I couldn't help smiling at the clothes hanging on the rows of racks in part of my four-thousand-square-foot townhouse. I was practically giddy from seeing my designs come to life right in front of my eyes.

Damn! I can't believe my collection is almost complete.

Rubbing my stiff neck with my fingers, I longed for a soak in a hot tub of lavender-scented bath salts, which was unlikely to happen tonight. I had been working nonstop for days. It had been both exciting and exhausting. There were moments when the stress from pushing myself so hard had driven me to near breaking point, but I'd continued. It had been a challenge, but it was my dream. It was make-or-break time, and I had no intention of failing.

I had designed around twenty different outfits, ranging from shredded organza dresses with flowers at the hem, cobweb gowns fluttering from neck to floor, crystal tank tops over short sequined skirts, to peacock-print silk dresses tumbling off one shoulder. But there were five more over-the-top pieces to go.

Shit.

I needed to work faster, but I was getting sidetracked by all the small details, like checking email, making phone calls, and keeping track of upcoming meetings.

Picking up my cell, I scrolled through my contacts, stopping on my as-needed intern. She was a whiz at helping me get as organized as possible.

"Hi, Sin. Great to hear from you. What's up?"

"Help! I'm up to my elbows in fabric."

Giselle laughed. "Whatever you need. I've been waiting for your call."

I sighed. "Things have gotten really complicated recently. The good news is I just got the thumbs-up from my business partner to hire extra help."

"When do you need me?" Giselle posed.

I flicked through the calendar on my tablet. "Today's already Friday. I'll give you the weekend to rest up and get ready to start working your ass off on Monday. We'll be working twenty-four seven, so be prepared to spend the night when needed. I have five more pieces I need to complete before I sit down with the buying and marketing teams to decide which designs will make the final cut." I made it sound simple, but eliminating designs would be a tiring process, involving fitting sessions and making alterations to clothes when needed.

But I eagerly anticipated the final stage—when my collection would go on sale.

"I'm so excited," Giselle squealed. "See you on Monday."

I sat down at my workstation. "Thanks, Giselle."

One more task was checked off my mounting to-do list, but it seemed like the more I accomplished, the more I added.

Trying to calm the anxious ball of energy bouncing around in my gut, I took a deep, cleansing breath. It didn't help. I jumped up, pulling my hair into a tight ponytail while pacing back and forth.

What the hell is wrong with me?

Things were going exactly the way I wanted. Finally.

Then a scary thought flashed through my head. I knew exactly what was wrong.

Core McKay.

Dammit.

Something had to give before I lost my ever-loving mind.

I had been masturbating nonstop, like a raging hormonal high schooler, but it still hadn't been enough to sate the palpable desire to fuck him senseless. Maybe Jade was right. I should just concede to my base urges and have sex with him. Yep, one hard round of hot and sweaty fucking would be enough to extinguish this insane fixation.

My cell buzzed.

"Hello?" I answered.

"Hello, Sin," Core responded in that wickedly sexy voice that always seemed to make my cunt clench, hard.

I cleared my throat. "What do you want, Core?"

"You on my bed with my face between your gorgeous legs."

The words, the sheer certainty in his rich voice, sent heat stabbing through me. *Shit. I'm seriously in lust with this man.*

"Not going to happen, Core."

He laughed. "Yet."

There was a fluttering in my stomach. "Ever," I finished.

"And just when things were going so well between us, you have to turn this into a fight."

"I'm working," I snapped with way more harshness than intended.

"I'm sending over a surprise for you."

My body stilled. "I don't like surprises." My pounding heartbeat grew loud in my ears.

He laughed huskily. "Liar."

I grimaced. "You know you're an ass, right?"

My doorbell rang.

"So I've been told," he responded dryly. "Go answer the door."

The line went dead.

Prowling over to the door with anxiousness and anticipation curled up in the pit of my stomach, I peered through the peephole. Standing at my door was a woman with sleek, flaming-red tresses left loose around her shoulders. Opening the door, I was stunned by her striking facial features—her dark autumn skin tone contrasted with her red hair, giving her an exotic vibe. Her eyes were shielded by aviators.

"Yes?" I asked, shaking myself out of my blossoming girl crush.

The woman whipped off her sunglasses, smiling impishly. "Sin Michaels?"

I cocked my head to the side. "Uh-huh."

Her almond-shaped black eyes lit with a twinkle of mischief. "I must say, you're even more gorgeous in person."

Arching a brow, I said, "Thank you?"

She stuck out her hand. "I'm Zuri, Core McKay's well-paid minion."

"Okay." Backing away, I eyed her hand like it was a snake.

Zuri shrugged before letting it drop.

"So what does my lord and master want now? A pint of blood? My firstborn?"

Zuri responded with a husky laugh. "Nope. Just your undying obedience to the king."

"Ain't happening."

"Wow. I think you and I are going to be besties. Can I come in?" she pleaded huskily.

I ran my eyes over her while rubbing an ear.

"Pretty please?" Zuri pouted playfully.

I gestured her in. "Sure."

A genuine smile lit up her face before she strutted past me, working skintight jeans and an off-the-shoulder black top. Her outfit was teamed with a mini top-handle bag, a small black shopping bag, and chic ankle boots. Essentially, she resembled a celebrity who had just jetted in from London. And I looked like death warmed over with my scrubbed-clean face and dark circles under my eyes.

She sucked in a quick breath. "Wow, beautiful place, Sin." Arching down, she brushed her fingers across the old worn trunk positioned next to my workstation like an accent piece. "Vintage?"

"No." I laughed. "Just some ratty old trunk that used to belong to my father."

Zuri stood up. "Things of sentimental value are always the most treasured pieces. Reminds you of where you've come from."

I smiled slightly. "So true."

Dad's trunk used to evoke all the sad memories associated with losing him so suddenly. But after years of mourning his loss, I'd decided to celebrate his life by pulling it out of hiding from the closet in my guest bedroom. Now, I admired it every day. It was a source of inspiration to never give up on my dream of making my collection a reality. Dad would have wanted me to be happy and successful, both in life and in business. His trunk was that constant reminder.

"My dad's trunk had more of an interesting life than most people I know. It was dragged around the country to every place we moved to."

The scratched leather was so worn and dirty that I couldn't tell the original color.

"Sounds like happy family memories. I wish we all could be that lucky," Zuri remarked in a monotone voice. Suddenly, she swayed over to the racks of hanging clothes. "Sin," she squealed dramatically. "You're the fucking Michelangelo of fashion." She touched the red cable-knit dress with a bustle and swath of chiffon peeking naughtily from its backside. "I've never seen anything this spectacular." She twirled to face me with a wide smile. "I can't wait to buy every damn piece."

"Thanks." Warmth radiated throughout my body. My collection was an homage to my twisted sensibility and willful disregard of conventional fashion. They were pieces designed by a woman, not a man's fantasy of women.

With raised eyebrows, she asked, "Is your collection complete?"

"Nope. I have five more pieces to go," I replied before padding over to the kitchen and grabbing a bottle of sparkling water from the refrigerator. "Would you like one?"

"No, thanks." Zuri moved away from my work area, surveying my townhouse. Without invitation, she sank down onto my favorite chaise, crossing her long legs and making herself at home.

I leaned a hip against the kitchen counter, and Zuri and I watched each other silently. Strangely, it wasn't a tense and awkward moment. It was more of a should-I-like-you analysis. Grudgingly, I concluded that I liked her so far. She nodded and smiled as if she'd also come to the same conclusion about me.

"So, Zuri, why are you here?"

"Honestly?" She pursed her bright-red pouty lips. "I just had to meet the woman who has Core all grumpy and sexually frustrated."

I strode over, sitting down in the plush chair directly across from her. "I'm pretty sure that fucker is always grumpy." I curled my feet under me. "And sexually frustrated? I highly doubt it. He looks like he gets knee-deep in pussy on a pretty regular basis."

"Fucker?" Zuri burst out laughing. "Wait till I tell the team Core has a new nickname." She chortled so hard a tear trickled at the corner of her eye.

I shrugged. "Just call it as I see it."

She sobered up. "But the knee-deep in sex part is totally off base. Well, at least recently." Her eyes twinkled. She snapped her fingers. "Oh, I almost forgot the real reason for my visit. Over there."

She gestured to the bag next to my chair. It was a small black shopping bag from an expensive and exclusive boutique in SoHo that catered to ultra-rich socialites and edgy celebrities. It wasn't unusual to see clothes from there on the red carpet. It was also a boutique I absolutely loved.

"It's a gift from Core."

"What type of gift?" My chest tightened.

Zuri's eyes gleamed. "Open it and find out."

The interior of my mouth went dry as I grabbed the bag. Reaching in, I pulled out an entirely translucent dress. I gasped. It was the dress I had drooled over when I first saw it in my favorite fashion magazine. I just couldn't rationalize paying the exorbitant price tag. Standing up, I held the knee-length backless mesh ensemble against my body. The dress was a little bit scandalous. Just fishnet and crystals and a couple of fingers crossed. I loved everything about it.

"Is it the correct size?" Zuri leaned forward.

Peeking at the tag, my pulse raced. "Surprisingly, yes, but how did you—"

"Me? No," she interrupted. "Core picked out the dress."

As I traced my fingers over the dress, there was a lightness in my chest. "I'm not sure—"

Zuri sighed heavily. "Girl, please don't say you're refusing that dress of absolute perfection."

"Oh, I'm accepting it." I laughed throatily. "I'm not fucking crazy. I've been stalking this dress for a while. What I meant was I'm just not sure why Core sent it." It was the truth. I had no intention of sending the dress back. I wanted it. Badly.

"There's a note inside the bag."

Digging inside the bag and pulling out the stark-white card, I read it aloud, "My driver will be at your house tonight at 10:30 p.m. sharp. C.M." Snorting, I tossed the card back inside the bag. "Well, what he wants and what he'll get are two different damn things."

"What Core wants, Core gets. Believe me." She smiled devilishly. "Must be that alpha-crazy thing he's got going on."

I drummed my foot against the floor. "And exactly where is Core taking me?"

"You've been cordially invited to the McKay Club's private playground, Noire."

Adrenaline rushed through my body. "A fancy name for the anything-goes section."

She winked at me. "More like anything you want."

"So I've heard from the gossip hags."

"Sweetie, the gossip is nowhere near the reality of Noire. It's total sexual chaos." Her cell beeped. She pulled it out of her handbag, gazing at it with a frown before she tapped out a text. "I've got to go." She stood up, flipping her hair over her shoulder. "I'll see you tonight."

"Wait a minute." My voice wavered. "I didn't say I was going."

A knowing smile curved Zuri's full lips. "Sin, that twinkle of excitement in your eyes says it all." She winked at me. "See you tonight," she finished before gliding away.

❧ *6* ❧

SINTHIA

I MUMBLED ALOUD, "I'm just going to play nice with Core, but absolutely no sex."

Leaning against my vanity with my fingers trembling, I finished my makeup with a bold red lip and eyes decorated in catlike flicks. And just when I thought I'd actually convinced myself about my no-sex rule, a vision of Core's hands snaking up my thighs and spreading them wide flashed through my mind.

"Dammit." I slammed my palm against the cold granite.

Who am I fooling?

I was most definitely going to have sex with him tonight—but just one round of toe-curling sex, nothing more. I couldn't allow myself to hope for more. I had been down that road before, picking up the pieces from hurt and heartache. I gritted my teeth. I had no intention of living through that car wreck ever again.

Stepping back, I smiled prettily at the mirror while clasping the silver bracelet Dad gave me for my birthday around my wrist before marching into my bedroom. I eyed the gorgeous dress lying across the bed. It was most definitely a dress picked out by a lover. The thought of Core selecting the dress with my body in mind made the liquid heat rage between my thighs.

After slipping on my flesh-toned thong, I skipped wearing a bra. It would stick out like a sore thumb in this barely there slinky, sheer number. Thank God the bodice of the dress was designed to pull up the voluptuous swell of my breasts, similar to the support of a bra. I slid the dress over my head, and it glided down my body like heavy silk. Giving myself a once-over in the mirror, I fell in love with the dress all over again. It was sexy and naughty, and it embodied the persona I needed tonight.

Seductress on the prowl.

Man-eater.

Woman ready to take Core by the balls...literally.

~

I STRODE OUT OF MY TOWNHOUSE AND DOWN THE STAIRS toward the driver waiting patiently while leaning against a sleek black limo.

He pushed away, tilting his head toward me. "Good evening, Ms. Michaels." He studied at me from head to toe with an appreciative gleam in his eyes while opening the back door.

"Thank you," I replied, maneuvering into the limo.

Shutting the door, he scampered around to the driver's side before sliding in.

"My name is Ace," he offered before turning the key and revving the engine.

"Hi, Ace," I returned before staring through the window, watching him drive smoothly into the Manhattan traffic.

After a few minutes of zipping in and out of the snarl of taxicabs and buses, Ace pulled up in front of the McKay Club.

Anxiously, I smoothed out the nonexistent wrinkles in my dress, waiting for Ace to open my door. Stepping out, I bit my bottom lip while staring at the nondescript warehouse that didn't have any of the fanfare of other clubs of this caliber. No lines were queued up behind the red velvet rope.

"Have a good time, Ms. Michaels."

"Thanks, Ace," I said before strutting up to a man wearing smart business attire and a clear Secret Service earpiece.

"Welcome to the McKay Club, Ms. Michaels." He greeted me as if he'd been waiting all night to see me. "When you step into the lobby, you'll find our door host stationed directly in front of the entrance to Noire." He gestured toward my wrist and then placed a black wristband around it before stepping aside.

"Thank you," I responded before entering the club.

I surveyed the scene, which was a little different from the last time I'd visited. The lobby was lit with what must have been thousands of candles. My gaze wandered to the man standing guard before an entrance draped with expensive-looking fabric as a guest flashed a black-and-gold wristband.

The door host shook his head. "Sorry. This area is members only."

Advancing across the space, the door host glanced down at my ink-black wristband and promptly stepped aside with a, "Noire is down the stairs." He pulled aside the fabric, allowing me entry.

The softly lit corridor with a sloped, mirrored ceiling and dark brick walls was different from anything I'd seen.

My stomach fluttered with anticipation as I thought of what lay ahead. With my sky-high heels tapping down the mirror-lined staircase, it didn't take me long to reach the Noire lounge. Immediately, I was attracted to the dazzling bar that encircled an illuminated champagne tower, and I decided to head toward it.

Once firmly planted in front of it, I beckoned the bartender. "Moscato and vodka."

He nodded before scampering away.

Tapping my foot to the music, I glanced around, stopping at the DJ tucked artfully in the corner. The dance floor was crowded with barely dressed bodies gyrating to the hard-hitting beat. Guests on the catwalk and semi-private second-floor mezzanine seating area eyed the partiers below. The multilevel space was like eye candy. Scantily dressed servers flittered around the edges of the dance floor, holding trays of champagne, mints, and condoms. I scanned around to my right, and nestled around the perimeter of the main level were harem-like tented booths draped with luxurious heavy silk fabric.

My breath hitched when I saw a blond woman I recognized from a popular television show leading a half-naked buff man by the hand into one of the tents. Normally, I would have felt like a total pervert watching the couple, but I knew this was the whole point of Noire—to watch and be watched. So like a deer in headlights, I gawked as the curvy blonde motioned him to his knees. Balancing on one leg, she flipped her other leg over his shoulder while he wrapped an arm around her waist to steady her, and then he leaned forward, devouring her center like he hadn't eaten in days.

"Holy shit," I mumbled under my breath.

So engrossed in the sexual antics, I hadn't even noticed Zuri's approach until she was standing directly in my path with a champagne flute in her hand. Leggy Zuri had donned a patterned cutout leather dress and teamed it with cerulean shoes.

Letting out a loud breath, I gestured for her to move aside. "Zuri, you're interrupting the best sex show ever."

Zuri scooted to my side. "So I see you're enjoying the sexcapade."

The couple had closed the tent.

"I was."

Not that I was into public sex-play myself, but I respected the boldness of others who got off on it.

I felt a soft tap on my shoulder. Peeping over it, I saw the bartender staring at me.

"Your drink." He smiled at Zuri. "Hi, Zuri."

"Hey, Scott. This is Sin. She's Core's guest. Give her anything her heart desires."

"Got it," Scott replied before hustling over to a beckoning guest.

Picking up my drink, I pressed my back against the bar. I didn't want to miss a single thing. Sipping the contents in my glass, I eyed Zuri, who was swaying seductively to the music with her cloud of shiny red hair floating around her.

"By the way, welcome to Noire." She gave me an impish grin. "I'm loving that dress on you."

"What can I say? Core does know the way to my heart. A fuck-me dress gets me every time."

Sipping my drink, I glanced around the club, pretending not to be searching for Core. My body pulsed with arousal when I found him making his way through the crowd. Biting my bottom lip, I gave him a slow once-over.

"Damn, he sure knows how to make cunts wet without even trying," I blurted.

Even among the gorgeous men littering the room, Core didn't blend. He stood out like a sexy marauding Viking, ready to conquer, destroy, and fuck any woman in his path.

I ached to be that woman.

"That he does," Zuri responded.

And as if he felt me eye-fucking him, he pivoted, staring at me, his eyes smoldering with intensity. Shamelessly, I drank in the magnificence of Core like a thirsty woman in a desert. My heart was beating like I'd just run fifty miles in thirty seconds while Core observed me.

Damn, I want to lick every inch of him.

Three words described Core—hotness and dripping sex. From his black tailored slacks that molded over his sculptured thighs to the crisp black shirt that fit across his magnificent, broad chest, I knew without a doubt there would be no denying him, no running away from the inevitable. I was going to fuck Core. My panties soaked and nipples hard as rocks, with deliberate effort, I broke eye contact with him.

Zuri stared at me. "Jesus, you do like him."

I eyed her right back. "No comment."

"There's no shame in admitting it. He's hot but a little rough around the edges." She pursed her full lips.

"A little?" I arched a brow. "You mean a lot."

Zuri shrugged. "He's not perfect, but none of us is."

I took a sip of my drink. "So how long have you been... working for him?"

Zuri snorted. "Is that your polite way of asking me if I've ever fucked him?"

I arched a brow. "Yep."

"We've never had sex. Truth be told, I've never thought of him that way. And he considers me to be a pain-in-the-ass baby sister."

Glancing back at him, I bit my lower lip, pondering why I gave a shit who he'd fucked. Then a horrible thought flashed through my head. *Exactly how many women has Core sent invitations and dresses to?* "Lots of women," I muttered, my stomach hardening.

Zuri eyed me shrewdly. "I know what you're thinking, and it's not like that. Core is very picky."

I wasn't quite sure if I believed that, but so far, Zuri had been straight up with me. Butterflies fluttered in my stomach. Needing all the liquid courage I could muster, I drained my glass and waited for his approach. But then the unthinkable happened. Core strode away.

My breath hitched before turning to Zuri. "Where the fuck is he going?"

Zuri's grin flickered so quickly I almost didn't see it. "It seems like Core wants you to come over and play." It was a statement more than a question.

My heart raced with excitement at the thought of pursuing Core like most men I'd desired. The problem was he wasn't most men. He wouldn't allow me to use him like a one-night stand or fucktoy. No, the rules of engagement between Core and me would be way different.

I flushed angrily. "There is no way I'm fucking him in public. I like my sexual encounters to be private."

Zuri chuckled. "So does he."

I pressed my lips together in a slight grimace. "That's surprising." I watched for any signs of deceit before laying my cards on the table. "Let's cut to the chase, Zuri. You know him way better than I do, and frankly, I'm way out of my depth right now, so—"

Zuri tilted her head. "You're asking for advice?"

"Yes."

"It's simple." Zuri shrugged. "If you want him, then hightail your sexy ass over there and get him."

"Seems deceptively simple," I responded with a weighted sigh.

Core was a predator, an alpha, savvy and calculating in everything he did, but it was too fucking late for me to walk away. Our fates had been sealed from the first moment we met.

Core and I were inevitable.

She offered a bemused smile. "Most things worth having are."

I licked my bottom lip, contemplating my next move while watching Core slice through the Noire crowd. He stopped to speak to several people. A woman boldly touched his arm. He ignored her, making a beeline through the elite crowd and stepping toward the waiting elevator guarded by two men. He said something to one, who eyed me and nodded before Core disappeared inside the closing elevator.

Zuri smiled. "Go on. He'll be waiting for you up in his VIP suite."

"What does he like?" I asked bluntly.

Zuri sipped her champagne. "Results."

❧ 7 ❧

SINTHIA

WITH NO FURTHER WORDS, I placed my glass on the bar and weaved my way across the dance floor. The sultriness of the air was palpable as bodies pressed against each other in unabashed lust and hedonism. Threesomes, women kissing women, men licking and sucking men, nude bodies slick from the heat of the pulsating energy surrounding them—it was sexual indulgence with no judgment.

Continuing my trek, I stood before the two highly visible men stationed by the elevator.

"Hello, Ms. Michaels," they greeted in unison. One gently ushered me into the elevator, while the other pressed a button on the control panel. "Upstairs is McKay's VIP suite. Just step out of the elevator. The entire suite is all one level."

The sound of music was silenced by the closing door. The ride to Core's suite was short, and the door slid open with a ding. I stepped off the elevator and landed in the opulent area before proceeding farther. I sucked in several deep breaths to calm myself when I saw Core sitting on the edge of a huge desk. His sleeves were rolled up, displaying his well-defined, tattooed forearms. My knees almost buckled from his sheer perfection.

Shit, no man should exude so much sex appeal.

Core was dark, hard, deadly, and absolutely yummy. A strange tingling sensation gripped my body like a vise as I fantasized about Core with his clothes off, my wrists pinned down by his big, powerful hands, and my legs curved around his waist while he fucked me until I blacked out.

God, I can't wait to see him completely nude.

He widened his long legs, giving me a once-over. "You're so fucking beautiful." His voice rumbled.

My body quivered with a desire I'd never felt before. "I've been called many things—exotic, hot, sexy—but never beautiful."

He slowly appraised my body. "Real beauty is quiet. The women I find most beautiful are the ones who aren't trying."

My stomach flip-flopped from the deepness of his words. They were both raw and sincere.

Damn, Core is a side of sexy trouble.

"And you in that dress is simply perfection. Now all I can think about is pulling it up and slipping my cock into your wet cunt."

My mouth dropped open as I took in a harsh breath. The vision of me naked, spread-eagled on his bed, his sexy gray eyes glazed over with lust made my folds warm and moist.

"Fuck, that's hot." My breathless response slipped out before I could stop it.

Silently, Core examined me but made no attempt to move from the edge of the desk. He was like a tiger stalking his prey, and for the first time in my life, I felt uncomfortable and unde-cided about my next move.

Embarrassingly, most of my previous sexual encounters had been fast and hard with no foreplay required. Pretty much wham, bam, thank you, ma'am. But I suspected Core expected a lot more from me.

I squeezed my eyes shut, trying to channel the anxiety out of my body. When that didn't work, I swayed over to the floor-to-ceiling window. Peering through the glass, I realized the vantage point gave me an excellent view of everything in Noire. It was Core's very own peep show. My eyes darted to the catwalk and then did a double take at the lone couple standing on it. Their bodies were wrapped around each other, and mouths were licking and sucking in the most erotic kiss I'd ever seen.

"Can they see in here?" I inquired.

"It's custom glass. We can see out, but they cannot see in." There was a long pause. "Having second thoughts, darling?"

"None," I replied before feeling the heat from Core's body behind me.

"If you decide to stay, either you're a hundred percent in, or you're out."

He was dark and all-consuming. He was everything I shouldn't want in a man, but damn, I craved him.

"Unlike our business arrangement, this partnership will be fifty-fifty, Core."

"Deal," he hissed against my ear before strong hands gripped my hips, yanking me against his chest. His alluring scent of amber and sandalwood engulfed me.

Biting my lip, I forced myself to focus on the passionate couple. The man pulled away from the woman. He reached for his belt, and he opened it frantically. Reaching inside, he pulled his arousal free as the woman's knees hit the ground. His hips thrust forward, and his cock pushed between her lips.

Core shifted his stance. His thighs spread wide on either side of my legs. "Do you like watching, Sin?" His lips kissed my neck, and his sharp teeth nipped the sensitive skin.

My mind whispered, *Yes*.

But it wasn't just the act of watching. It was Core's presence and the way his hard body felt pressed against mine. My head arched back, resting against his hard chest. A wave of arousal washed over me when his hands squeezed my hips. His firm male heat nudged against the small of my back.

"You see how she's enjoying having him in her mouth? There's no force. He's letting her take what she needs."

Slowly, he moved one hand from my hip, using it to trace a finger across my wet lips. "Has your mouth ever been taken?"

A delicious shiver of arousal ran down my spine. "Yes," I whispered before my tongue darted out to lick the pad of his callused finger.

He slid his finger between my lips, moving it in and out. "But with me, your mouth will be a virgin." His finger stilled before falling away. "Watch them, Sin," Core commanded.

I pushed my head back up, and through slitted eyes, I centered on the woman sensually deep-throating her lover. A moan escaped my lips as Core grabbed both my hands, spreading them against the cool glass like it was a stickup.

"Do you want to suck my cock, Sin?"

His seductive words made me inhale sharply. His touch, his smell, his voice were driving me toward the edge of sheer sensual insanity. Bit by bit, I was losing control to him.

"Yes," I hissed. Moisture trickled between my legs. My hips surged forward and then back.

He chuckled wickedly, dropping his hand from on top of mine. I bit back a whimper of lust as Core's hand traced my areolae and taut nipples, trailing his fingers back and forth over the peaks, pinching them hard. His every touch felt hardwired to my core. I wanted to come right on the spot. I'd never had anyone do something so erotic to me.

My hips rolled as I neared orgasm.

"Beg to suck my cock, Sin." The command in his voice was obvious.

Lust and fear curled into my stomach. It sent ripples of desire rushing through my body. Effortlessly, Core was dominating me.

"I can't think—" My voice was barely over a whisper.

Dropping his hand from my breast, he burrowed his fingers into my hair, yanking my head back. "Listen to your body," he growled into my ear.

My sex flexed as his grip tightened. Sexual desire coiled so hard that my stomach spasmed.

His breath caressed my neck. "I want you to crave the feel of my hard cock fucking your mouth."

The power of his words literally made my knees buckle. Core rotated me to face him. I shivered from the coolness of the glass pressed against my back.

My breath stopped at the intense hunger in his eyes as he stroked a finger down my cheek, trailing to my bottom lip. I jerked at the contact.

"Don't move," he ordered. "I will give you what you need, not what you want."

He slid his hands to my jaw, and he tilted his head before settling his lips across my mouth. My breath caught. His grip on my jaw contracted. He slid his tongue between my teeth. His kiss was long, slow, and deep—the stamp of his possession. No one had ever kissed me like this.

Jesus, I'm so fucked.

He sucked my tongue into his mouth. My stomach contracted as a rush of heat flooded my entire body. My hands wrapped tightly around his lean waist. Lust curled deep into my damp, moist, needy place. Core was slowly crumbling my resolve to remain emotionally detached.

He pulled his lips away from mine but kept his hand firmly controlling my head. He smiled like the devil reincarnated. In one sinuous motion, he released his hold and tugged up the hem of my dress, clutching both of my ass cheeks.

I leaned up, my teeth grazing his throat, before I inched back ever so slightly. Releasing one hand from his waist, I grazed his face with the backs of my fingers, moving from his cheek to his full lips. As I caressed his chiseled mouth with my fingers, he opened his lips and licked my knuckle with just a quick flick of his warm tongue. A feeling of excitement fluttered like butter-flies in the pit of my stomach. The sensation ratcheted up my emotions like a kid on a roller coaster.

He fastened his mouth on mine. My womanhood was drenched, with everything inside me shattering from his kiss. I desperately clutched his shoulders with my hand to anchor myself. My soft lips were on his hard ones. A stinging nip of his teeth made me open my mouth, and he plunged in, his tongue stroking mine.

There was no gentleness in Core. That trait should have sent me stampeding away, but instead, like a junkie, it heightened my insatiable need to submit to him. I dug my nails into his muscular shoulder as the searing need burned between my legs.

Nudging my legs apart, he moved between them. With his hands on my ass, he slid me closer until my sex rubbed across the aching bulge in his pants. Our kiss deepened. I rubbed against his hard-on with a slow and steady motion.

Dropping his hold on me, he said, "Sin, get on your knees." His voice was deep and caressing, sliding across my skin like silk.

My stomach rolled with anxiousness as I leaped into the pits of scorching hell and slid to my knees. With trembling fingers, I unbuckled his belt and unzipped his pants.

Sweet Jesus, no underwear.

He stared at me with his penetrating gaze. "Release my cock."

I shivered as I touched his hardness. He was long and beautifully thick. When he was all out, I stroked him gently.

"Damn," I whispered.

He was the epitome of fucking masculine perfection. His engorged, thick manhood stretched taut, almost past his navel. The thick, round crown glistened with a small drop of moisture. His balls were tight with arousal.

My cunt tingled, and my peaks puckered as I craved the salty taste of him. Aggressively, I grabbed his manhood with both hands, feeling the hardness swell. Massaging the smooth, hot column of flesh between my fingers, I leaned forward to take the swollen head into my greedy mouth when he grasped my hair, snatching my head back.

Our eyes locked.

"Ask for permission." He kept his voice low and soft but left no room for doubt that he'd issued an order.

My jaw dropped. "What?"

"You heard me."

I tried to get away from his grasp, but his fingers tightened.

"Ask politely, Sin." His voice was more of a drawl with a definite hint of seduction at the end.

I raised my chin in a gesture of defiance. "No."

"Sin, let's not play games." His voice was deep and held just a tinge of irritation. "Beg for it. Out loud. I want your utter surrender."

I pasted a smile on my face and delivered my next line in a saccharine-sweet tone, "No matter how spectacular your cock is"—*and it was*—"that shit is not happening."

His mouth compressed into a hard line. "We'll go no further if you don't trust me to give you what you need." His eyes narrowed and his nostrils flared.

My body shivered at his words. *Can he really give me what I've been too jaded to believe existed?* A man who understood my needs behind closed doors and would satisfy all the dark cravings I'd kept buried. Deep down, I knew he was that man, but I couldn't quite push past the fear of surrendering to him.

"I can't," I whispered.

He cocked a brow at me. "Can't? Or won't?"

My pulse accelerated at his question, and my eyes narrowed as he did the unthinkable. He stepped back and started stroking his engorged manhood tauntingly.

Dammit! What a cunt tease.

It was straight-up torture as I watched the way he touched himself. Nothing screamed confidence more than a man not afraid of tantalizing his sensual side. My breath became more ragged. Warmth pooled between my thighs. I was so close to the edge that I wasn't above begging for his shaft. And from the smoldering calculation in his gray eyes, Core knew it.

Stubbornly, I ran through multiple scenarios in my head. *One, tell him to go fuck himself, go home, and finish myself off with my trusty and reliable vibrator, Beast. Or two, beg for the privilege of taking him down my throat.* Option one would never satisfy me now that I'd had a glimpse of his hard flesh. Option two... *Oh, hell no.* I'd never had to beg to take a man into my mouth in my entire life.

His stroke became more sensual, slower and methodical.

Shit. He's trying to drive me insane.

I blew out a breath. "Please, Core." I bit my lip and quickly added, "May I suck your cock?"

His stoic expression turned grim. "No." Steel laced his tone.

I stiffened at his response. *Motherfucker!* I swiveled my head, unable to meet his tauntingly hot gaze.

"But you may lick it. Slowly." His voice was full of authority.

I forced myself to gaze at him again. I tightened my fists.

His lips twitched into a mockery of a smile.

I squared my shoulders and took a deep breath. I grabbed his girth, feathering my tongue over him, swirling the salty precome from the tip of his crown, savoring the earthy taste of him. Cupping his balls, I rolled my fingers over his tight sac. My other hand firmly gripping him, I explored the peaked ridge just under the head of his shaft with my tongue.

"Enough." His rough command drew me to a halt.

I let out a strangled cry. My chest heaved as I rested my head against his hard thigh.

His hand ventured to the back of my head. He tugged my hair with his fingers, forcing my gaze upward. "Let me show you how I want my cock sucked." His tone was edgy. "Open your mouth."

His command made my insides tingle. No man had ever talked to me that way. He was pushing my limits, breaking me down, taking everything I'd worked so hard to maintain...to control.

I embraced his length with both hands before my lips greedily slid over the head of his arousal. Core's hands threaded through my hair, as though savoring the feel of it. The low groans coming from him spurred me on.

He tightened his hand, jerking my hair. He grew bigger in my mouth as I bobbed my head up and down over his wide shaft. The more I tasted, the more I hungered. With every flick of my tongue, the hard grip of his fingers against my head seemed to turn me on even more. I fed him into my throat, taking it all. His hard shaft was thick and broad, like him. My lips stretched around his man flesh.

He spread his knees wider. "That's it. Suck me good."

I hummed as he started a slow slide in and out between my lips.

A fog of desire clouded my vision. All I could think of was bringing him pleasure.

His groan deepened, becoming more of a growl, charging the erotic tension even more. "More tongue. Suck harder," he hissed.

His dark words sent me spiraling to the edge of a lust-induced frenzy. My body quivered with a fire I'd never felt before. I didn't give a shit about how wild he was making me or my running mascara or smudged lipstick.

I didn't think. I just felt liberated and bizarrely in control of Core.

I closed my eyes briefly, letting out a strangled sound. My tongue stroked every bump and ridge of his flesh. Moving up and down on him, I sucked him harder. I was thrilled when his hands moved to my head again, positioning me over his member.

"Wider." He tightened his fists even more in my hair. "Open your mouth wider."

I did, and he shoved his staff until he was lodged against the back of my throat. He was huge, the size of my wrist, but I didn't back away or struggle. Holding still, I relaxed my throat to keep from gagging. My tongue slid along his length as I breathed through my nose and swallowed around him.

"Fuck. Do that again." His voice was hoarse and thick with arousal.

Heady with power, I swallowed around him. The sound of his harsh breath filled the room. It drove me on as he thrust into me with a slow rhythm that was rough and primal. His tangled fingers in my hair held my head still for his deep thrusts.

Class was in session, and he was teaching me what he demanded. And like a good little student, I was eager to learn.

My lips danced over him. My hips swayed in tandem.

"Sinful," he whispered.

Moisture pooled between my legs, loving that he called me "sinful" when we got this nasty.

All too soon, a guttural groan erupted from his carnal mouth. "Swallow it all," he commanded a second before he shot into the sweet depths of my mouth.

I continued to suck, swallow, and lick him with gentle strokes until he gradually softened in my mouth.

After inching from between my lips with a heartfelt sigh, in one smooth motion, he helped me stand. My legs were trembling under me, and he cradled me against his chest with unexpected tenderness that left me speechless. My body jerked involuntarily, and a mental switch flipped from lust-induced haze to lucid reality. I'd never been held like this.

My body stiffened. I felt raw, exposed, and confused. *What the fuck am I doing?*

He stroked my hair. "Don't overthink this. Just feel," he coaxed.

I squeezed my eyes shut for a moment, trying to do the opposite of what he'd demanded. Feeling was exactly what had allowed me to get hurt by Kyle so many years ago. Feeling was what I'd sworn not to do because it hurt too damn much when my heart eventually got broken. And that was exactly what would happen with a man like Core.

No, it would be better to keep whatever we had strictly sexual. Sex, I understood. Relationships and emotions were not in my vocabulary.

My heartbeat raced, nearly exploding. "This is bullshit. I

don't want to fucking feel." My voice broke. I cleared my throat. "I want to fuck you and be done with all of this." I wanted him to get angry. I needed his rejection to fuel my will to hightail it away from him and away from this intimacy.

I needed him to save me from myself.

He stepped back and grabbed my chin roughly. His eyes were clear and determined. "It will never be done between us, Sin. You're mine. All of you."

Momentarily, I was unable to speak. "No." My voice trembled. "Friends with benefits."

The muscles jumped near his jawline. "I'll have all of you or none of you," he clipped out. "That's the only way it will be." He removed his hand from my chin, pinning me with his hardened eyes.

I held back a scream of frustration. My aching desire for him threatened to drown me.

His mouth compressed into a thin line. "Sin, you can waste a whole lot of time pretending this isn't happening, but it is. The sooner you come to terms with your new reality, with me in it, the sooner I can get to shoving my cock into your sweet pussy and fucking you sideways." His nostrils flared, and every muscle in his body seemed to tense. "But that's not going to happen until you surrender to me, in every way a woman can surrender to a man."

He brushed a hand against my breast and teased the tight bud of my nipple between his fingers. Liquid heat poured through me, and my stomach quivered.

Jesus.

The mere thought of surrendering to Core on an emotional level made me dizzy with fear. My hands started shaking. I swallowed hard and bit my bottom lip to hide the emotion that had set it trembling. Clamping my fingers together, I tried to remember how to breathe.

Emotionally, I was falling down the rabbit hole. It was dark, cold, and disorientating.

"What is this?" I'd meant to sound abrupt and firm, but the words came out kind of breathy.

He arched down, and his teeth grazed over my ear before sucking the lobe into his mouth, eliciting a gasp from me. "Like I just told you, you're mine. All of you. And you will submit to me in every way I see fit."

"Like fuck buddies?" I squeaked, feeling like I was losing my ever-loving mind.

"No." His expression was serious. "I want more than an occasional fuck. I can get that shit anywhere."

I almost swallowed my tongue. "Are you talking about us dating?" *Oh God.* I didn't know shit about dating.

He ran his tongue along the seam of my lips, tempting me to open for him. "I don't date. I fuck. That means me fucking you whenever I want, wherever I want, and however I want. Exclusively." He wrapped a strand of my hair around his finger and tugged. "Because I damn sure don't share or play nice with others."

Uh, what? My mind screamed, *Run*, but my body froze, allowing him to fondle my hair affectionately. *What the hell is wrong with me?* I'd never reacted to a man like this, no matter how hot he was.

I pursed my lips. "No. That's you acting like some big, bad junkyard dog, using me as your fucktoy and then discarding me when you're done."

"No. It's us satisfying our urge to fuck each other senseless —" his chiseled lips curled "—with the added bonus of spending quality time with each other, seeing where this goes."

My heart instantly began to race with elation, but my stubborn mind refused to budge. "Sounds a lot like fucking with a hell of a lot of non-fucking activities thrown in. The sex part sounds hella good. But I don't do bullshit outings to the park, holding hands, or rolling around on picnic blankets, getting grass stains on my clothes." I pinched my lips together.

It was all true. There wasn't a girlie or romantic bone in my body.

He arched a brow. "Do I look like the type of man who likes to traipse through the damn park?"

He smiled, an honest-to-God, naughty-boy smile. Disarmed, I shivered.

"My idea of romance is me finger-fucking you under the table at my favorite restaurant and then denying you the pleasure of climaxing."

Okay...that sounds really good. My traitorous center quivered with lust. Ignoring the danger warning blaring in my head, I whispered, "Core, we have a deal."

He slid his hand between my legs, rubbing against my wet folds. "Do we?" He arched his beautiful brow. "I have very dark tastes when it comes to sex. And I'm planning on exploring every one of them, leaving nothing unfucked. Including your ass."

His words made my stomach flutter with excitement. It was a primal challenge no man had ever made me want to answer. There were no flowery, bullshit words, no complicated promises of forever, no judgment for the freaky things we both craved. He'd push my sexual boundaries, maybe even strip me emotionally bare, ruining me for any man after him.

But I wanted Core for however long this thing between us might last.

"Like I said, Core. Deal."

His hands slid under my arms, lifting me effortlessly.

"What are you doing?" I squeaked, my dress twisting around my waist. Instinctively, I wrapped my arms around his neck and my legs around his waist.

"I'm getting ready to spread your legs wide open and lick your sweet slit, darling."

Striding across the floor, he carried me over to his desk. With one hand, he swiped everything off of it before sliding me on top. In the blink of an eye, I was on my back with my legs hooked over his shoulders. He settled himself between the V of my thighs, pushing my panties aside before voraciously going after the damp petals of my womanhood. He lapped me from my clit to the end of my cleft. He swirled his tongue around my clit, repeatedly flicked it, and then sank it inside me. I panted, my hips arching. Holding me still, he fucked me unrelentingly with his wicked tongue. I hissed as he worked me into a frenzy, using long, sensual licks. His tongue constantly teased my opening.

"Who does this pussy belong to?" he gritted out as he pinned me.

Showing me no damn mercy, he flicked my swollen nub with his tongue until I screamed, "Oh my fucking God!"

I bucked as he continued to bathe me with his mouth.

"Whose is it, Sin?" He thrust two fingers into my trembling channel, curving them inside me while pressing his thumb on my clit so his hand was clamped around me.

I knew he had no intentions of letting me come until I verbalized his claim. Frustrated, I was squirming helplessly and arching. "Technically, it's mine," I responded breathlessly.

He growled, the vibrations pushing me to the edge of crazed lust.

"But since you're doing such a bang-up job down there, I concede to your talented, wicked tongue. So lick away, Core."

He shoved another finger inside me, making me cry out and buck. "Concede to *me*, not my fucking tongue."

My toes curled. I was so close. Just one more swipe of his tongue. "Okay. This pussy is on loan to you on a very temporary basis."

"Don't make me smack your twat."

"You wouldn't." My mouth dropped open at the sharp slap against my slick clit. My nipples tightened with desire. "You—"

"Enough." He flicked my womanhood with his tongue. "Say the damn words, or I'll walk away, leaving your stubborn ass hanging."

I jerked my head up to stare at him. "What? You wouldn't?"

My voice held a tinge of hysteria. I was so wound up with the need to come, and shamefully, I wasn't above begging.

I needed Core. *Now.*

He raised his head, peering at me with sharpened eyes. My juices glistening on his lips like liquor filled me with perverse satisfaction and possessiveness.

"I would," he growled. "This won't work if I don't hear what I need." He stood up, and with his free hand, he pulled out his thickness, rubbing it tauntingly. "This cock is all yours."

I swallowed hard, watching as he stroked it sensually. His manhood was by far the thickest, largest, most perfectly shaped shaft I'd ever seen.

"And this pussy is mine." He plunged his fingers, hard, inside my aching wetness. "Yes?"

I nodded. All the while, it was killing me that I was conceding so quickly. But dammit, it was hard as hell to find a man in Manhattan with the Holy Grail—a huge dick and a very talented tongue.

I was greedy for more.

He narrowed his steel-gray eyes. "No nodding. I need to hear the fucking words, Sin."

Sealing my submission, I uttered, "It's yours. Take all of me."

With one seamless motion, he withdrew his fingers, gripped my ass, and stabbed his tongue inside me. My back arched, and my legs moved to the back of his head as I cried loudly for air to breathe. Consumed with lust, he continued to fuck me relentlessly with his tongue.

I reached my fingers down, biting into his silky hair while he pumped me, drawing out my climax. Pulling my ass cheeks apart, he plunged one wet finger into the normally forbidden zone— my ass. My eyes rolled to the back of my head. I panted, drawing ragged breaths. Mercifully, he relented, pulling away, his eyes blazing with a focused, animal wildness.

Holy hell.

I couldn't even form a coherent thought. Every muscle in my

body tensed with expectation. I was so horny that all I wanted was to fuck.

"Fuck me," I demanded, all cavewoman-like.

He growled before hauling me off the desk, holding me securely as my legs wobbled.

Light-headed, I closed my eyes to get my bearings.

"Open your eyes." His voice was taut with lust.

I hesitated. My body was a shuddering mass of jelly.

"Now, Sin." His voice hardened.

Trembling, I opened my eyes. His eyes were now dark gray, like molten silver.

"Strip." He widened his stance.

On shaky legs, I slowly slid my dress off my body and then pushed my panties down my hips and legs before kicking them aside. I stood before Core, wearing nothing but my sexy stilettos. Gliding my hands up, I cupped my cleavage before squeezing my hardened peaks between my fingers.

"Is that what you want, Sin? Pain?" He drew his lower lip between his teeth.

My whole body ached with longing. "I want it all."

"Sinful." He stripped off his shirt, leaving on his unzipped pants.

I caught myself staring and cleared my throat. His body, from chest to sleeve, was a wonderland of beautifully composed Japanese tattoos and other beast-themed ink. Stepping closer, he lifted my chin with a flick of his finger and kissed me hard and deep. It was a kiss of utter possession.

He broke off the exchange and growled, "Turn around, face-down, and present your beautiful ass to me. Now."

There was something different about his voice. The gruffness I had gotten used to was gone. There was a new tenderness that I hadn't heard before.

Pivoting, I pressed my chest against the desk. "Like this?"

The cool air glided across the backs of my thighs. He ran a hand across the curve of my ass before parting my cheeks. A strange tingling sensation gripped my body like a vise. My eyes shut at the revelation that Core was viewing me in ways that no other man had.

"Damn, you're so damn sexy," he praised while kicking my legs apart like I was under arrest.

With sweet lust whipping through my dripping sex, I glanced over my shoulder, and I watched him reach into his pocket and pull out a condom. He tore the package open with his teeth and quickly removed the latex.

In seconds, he sheathed his cock and curled his hand in my hair, snapping my head back. "Your pussy. Your ass. All of you. Mine," he whispered into my ear.

Releasing my hair, he pressed me facedown onto the desk and buried himself so far inside me that my whole body quaked from the sheer force.

"Oh fuck!" I cried out as he stretched me ruthlessly.

His engorged flesh sank deeper between my sensitive folds, and his balls slapped against my womanhood, sending tiny shocks through my body. My hips bucked, and my pussy burned from the width of his big, thick manhood.

With fingers buried into the flesh at my hips, he held me still. "Slow, darling. I don't want to hurt you." He gave my wetness time to adjust to his girth.

My body tensed from the burning fullness in my cunt.

"Relax," he hissed.

I took a deep breath, forcing my rebellious muscles to loosen.

He pushed forward, slowly at first, and then he increased his speed from a sensuous slide to hard, forceful pumping. "Fuck!" he cursed.

I couldn't move as Core rocked me, hard and steady. The feeling of helplessness ran through me, heightening every sensation in my body. He was driving me crazy with lust, and each stroke brought me closer and closer to the edge.

"Core," I groaned as he continued to fuck me like a man

possessed.

The pressure tightened inside me before I came brutally hard. I gasped and moaned as my interior muscles convulsed around him.

His fingers squeezed my hips. Again and again, he pulled out and plunged back inside me like a man on a mission. He tensed, and every muscle rippled before he uttered a guttural groan that sounded like, "Sinful," as his smooth pumping became jerky and harsh. He roared. His entire body shook as he came and came, his cock twitching inside me. He slumped over me, catching his weight on his hands. He nuzzled my neck and then pressed his sensuous mouth to the top of my shoulder before gently pulling out of me.

I sighed heavily, feeling utterly empty.

"Let me take care of the condom." He disappeared for a second to dispose of it.

When he came back, tremors ran through me as his lips trailed gently across the back of my neck, causing my stomach to do flip-flops. Twisting me around, he enveloped me with his body by wrapping his arms around me. Effortlessly, he picked me up, cradling me. Pressing my head into the hollow of his shoulder, he carried me over to the sitting area as if I weighed nothing. He sat down with me in his lap.

I felt safe and comforted. Boneless, I curled against his chest while he pushed the damp strands of hair away from my forehead. In that instant, I knew I had been stamped *Property of Core*. There would be no pretending this was just a one-time occurrence, and from the determined glint in his eyes, he wouldn't let me even if I wanted to. It was way too late in the game for that.

His chest was damp with sweat, slick under my cheek, salty on my tongue when I gave it a lick. Through the muscles covering his chest, I could hear his heart beating in a steady rhythm. He traced his fingers over the tattoo piece written horizontally from my abdomen to my back.

"Love all, trust a few, do wrong to none," he recited aloud. "Shakespeare," he ended.

I curved my mouth up into a smile. "Wow. I've never seen this side of you, Core."

His sensuous mouth twitched. "I have many sides, darling." His hand moved to my ass, lightly touching. "Good."

"Bad," I whispered.

"Hard." His voice rumbled through his chest as he stroked my hair.

"Gentle," I finished.

He arched a brow. "Gentle? I'm afraid not. Gentle is not in my vocabulary." He tweaked my nipple hard.

"I can deal with that." I traced my fingers along his jaw and across his lips.

He bit one finger before letting go. "I'll be right back," he muttered while gently scooting me off his lap before he stood up. Confidently, he swaggered over to the wet bar.

Lust curled in my cunt.

Damn, what a magnificent ass.

He stormed back with a tall glass of ice water. Without a word, he sat down, pulling me back onto his lap. Cradling me in his arms, he held the glass to my lips, and I drank thirstily. When I'd had enough, he drank some of the water.

"Do you want more?" he inquired, gesturing to the glass.

I shook my head. "No, I'm good."

Putting the glass down, he tucked a strand of my hair behind my ear, his fingers leaving a tingle in their wake. I tried to burrow closer, but I was already plastered against him like wallpaper. My chest was mashed against his, and my hips were cradled against his stomach.

Arching down, he crushed his lips against mine before pulling back. His gray eyes searched my face as if he were trying to figure out a puzzle, and I was that puzzle.

"For better or for worse, Sin, we're in this together."

✦ 8 ✦

SINTHIA

"Wake up, darling. We're here." Core's voice was low and sensuous.

I popped my eyes open to find him staring at me. "Sorry. I fell asleep." I was curled against Core's side, totally satiated after our energetic sex romp.

With languid movements, I stretched. He traced a finger across my cheek.

"What?" I wiped my eyes. "Did I snore?"

"No." He took my hand and turned it over so he could kiss my palm, the sensation making a beeline for my sex. "You just look so cute when you're sleeping and not spewing four-letter words."

He gently placed another kiss on my palm before licking it. His touch stabbed through me, and moisture pooled between my legs.

I smiled impishly. "Fuck off, Core."

He laughed huskily. "And there she is, my foul-mouthed sex kitten." He threw open the limo door and stepped out, holding his hand for me to grab. "Time to get you inside."

I clutched his hand, hopping out.

Releasing my hand, he pressed his palm to my lower back,

ushering me up the stairs. "So do I at least get to see where the fashion magic happens?"

I burst out in laughter. Turning around, I rolled my eyes heavenward. "Okay, is that your subtle way of asking to come inside and have your freaky, naughty way with me?"

He offered a bemused smile. "I didn't know I needed an invitation."

"With your talented cock, you can come over to service me anytime, Core." I leaned in, pecking him, before twirling around to resume my climb toward my front door. Pulling my key out of my mini clutch, I started to push the key into the lock when I noticed the door was already open with the lights on inside. A sense of dark foreboding weighed on me.

With shakiness in my limbs, I rushed forward, but Core yanked me back, pushing his muscular body in front of mine.

"Sin, let me go inside first." He nudged the door and stepped over the threshold. His body stiffened. "Holy shit!"

His wide, muscular back was blocking my view. "What?"

I shoved against him, but he refused to budge.

"Move the fuck out of my way, Core."

Slowly, he stepped aside, allowing me entry.

I froze, rooted to the spot.

It was like a tornado had ripped through my townhouse. Furniture had been slashed and thrown about. Kitchen drawers were pulled out. Broken glass and dishes littered the floor. Throw pillows had been cut, and down feathers were scattered everywhere. Nothing had been left untouched.

My lips trembled. "Who the fuck would do something as horrific as this?"

I was stunned into silence. My pulse raced as I continued my visual inventory. My flat-screen television and laptop were still there. I clasped my hands together to keep them from trembling, and my eyes widened when I saw the remnants of my collection ripped into pieces and thrown around like confetti.

"Oh God." My breathing sped up until I was gasping for air.

My legs gave way, and I felt myself crashing toward the floor when Core caught me.

His deep voice sounded from behind me. "Breathe, darling."

Unchecked tears streamed down my cheeks. "I don't understand what's happening right now." My voice broke as I shook uncontrollably.

He spun me around to face him, and his hands framed my jaws, anchoring me in place. "Sin, eyes on me. Calm down."

I forced myself to remain calm even though my insides screamed bloody murder.

He released me, righting a barstool that had been toppled onto the floor. "Sit down before you fall. I'll handle this." A muscle in his jaw twitched.

Shakily, I sank onto the chair, hooking my feet around the legs. Core stalked over to the refrigerator, pulling out a bottle of water. Wasting no time, he strode back, handing me the bottle.

I waved it away. "I'm not thirsty." My voice croaked as I set my palms down flat on the counter. My mind raced a mile a minute with questions. *What if I had been home? Would I be dead right now? Who the fuck would do something like this?*

He tucked a lock of my hair behind my ear. "Please drink it, darling."

I drew in a deep breath, taking the bottle with stiff fingers. Opening it, I sipped it absentmindedly.

"I need to call the police. Don't move." He kissed my forehead before pulling out his cell.

But I didn't care. All I could think about was how truly fucked my life was right now.

~

HOURS LATER, UNIFORMED AND PLAIN-CLOTHES POLICE officers stomped through my home.

Calming deep breaths, Sin, I chanted to keep myself from going completely insane.

After doing a walk-through with the police and Core, I could easily see the damage was worse than I'd originally thought. When pressed by the police to give an inventory of what had been stolen, I couldn't pinpoint what was missing. All my jewelry and other expensive items remained untouched. Not that I gave a shit. Material possessions could be replaced, but my collection could not. The intruder had ruthlessly destroyed it with a thoroughness that was mentally and emotionally disturbing.

Why would anyone do this?

I couldn't think of one competitor who hated me this much. My life was uncomplicated. There was no drama, no rivals. I frowned. But there was one man who had been following me from the past—after one night of sex, now he was my stalker.

Is Jaxon back to claim what he thinks is his—me?

My mind rejected the possibility, but the scary memory of the utter rage that had clouded Jaxon's eyes before he'd sliced my shoulder made me shudder. The all-too-familiar dread seeped into my bones. I gritted my teeth as I tried not to freak out.

Sin, stop it. He's gone.

But I knew he wasn't. The vase of white roses and the note with the letter *J* scribbled on it that had been left on my doorstep a couple weeks ago proved it.

My hand flew to the light scar on my shoulder. "Never forget," I whispered.

Fighting the cold fear running down my spine, I thought about the day Jaxon had grabbed me, pulling me into a dark alleyway, with a knife pressed against my throat.

He babbled words of love over and over as he brutally ripped off my clothes with sick lust in his eyes. Bitterness coated my tongue when I realized I was nothing but a piece of property to him, his possession that he had every intention of claiming over and over again until I broke. Tears streamed down my face as I braced for the impending savage violation. Shivering on the cold ground, I turned my head away, letting my mind go blank. Then a lone homeless man stumbled upon us, saving me, and I was thrown a lifeline. But I knew Jaxon wasn't finished with me, and that had just been a momentary reprieve.

My thoughts snapped back to the present. I shuddered. The break-in showed me just how vulnerable I really was. I'd never needed a security system in this affluent neighborhood, but getting one was the first thing on my agenda today.

Wandering back into the living room, I tried not to let my eyes linger on the pieces of my collection that lay in ruin across the floor.

"What the hell?" I muttered under my breath when I tripped over an object.

Glancing down, I toed the offending large chunk of old, splintered wood that had once covered the false bottom of Dad's beat-up trunk. The trunk was lying on its side with all the contents spilled out like seashells on a beach. Righting it, I scanned inside. The false bottom was missing, and so was the red leather ledger that had been hidden in the secret compartment.

Standing up, I scanned the entire area. *No ledger.* "This shit keeps getting stranger and stranger."

"Sin?" Core lifted an eyebrow, eyeing me from across the room. "Are you okay?"

"Yes, I'm good." I forced a smile.

Core glared at me with an intensity that made me uncomfortable before his gaze pivoted back and he continued talking to one of the officers.

I drew my lower lip between my teeth while staring at him.

A man I'd at one time thought of as my enemy was now my lover. Smoothly, Core had stepped in, taking charge of fielding the barrage of questions from the officers while I numbly rode a roller coaster of emotions—shock, fear, denial, and anger.

"Ms. Michaels?"

I snapped my head up at the sound of my name. A well-groomed, middle-aged man moved toward me.

"Yes?" I answered.

He adjusted the lapels of his jacket. "I'm Detective Talbot." His face flushed as he studied my attire with thinly veiled interest. "Seems like you were out when the break-in occurred." He furrowed his forehead. "You're very lucky."

"That's what everyone keeps telling me," I replied dryly.

Talbot inclined his head. "I do have some questions to ask you. First—"

I massaged the back of my neck. I'd had enough of the questions. I was exhausted, mentally and physically. I sighed with relief when Core sidled up, wrapping an arm around my waist.

"We've already been through the scene with your officers," Core interjected.

"And who are you?" Talbot's voice was clipped, as if he were irritated.

Core let out a harsh breath. "Core McKay," he snapped. "Now, no more questions. She's in shock. Can't this wait until later today?"

Talbot scrutinized me and then nodded slowly. "Sure." He turned to face Core. "Just make sure you bring her to the station today." He gestured toward the officers. "Come on, guys. Let's clear out." He pivoted and marched out the door, closing it behind him.

Core swiveled me around to face him. "Are you okay?"

"No." Feeling raw and vulnerable, I wrapped my arms around his waist. "I'm so totally screwed, Core." I gulped hard so I wouldn't lose my voice. "My collection is gone. I'll have to start all over again."

"Whatever you want and need, I'll move mountains to make sure you have it, darling." He kissed my forehead and whispered, "But right now, I need you to gather whatever is salvageable. You're staying with me until we get this whole thing sorted out."

I buried my face into his chest. In Core's arms, I felt safe.

9

CORE

DISGUST TWISTED my mouth into a sneer. I still couldn't believe Jeff had destroyed Sin's house. I gnashed my teeth as I climbed the stairs. I couldn't wait to get over to the warehouse and wrap my hands around his neck, watching the life slowly drain from his eyes. Reaching the top of the landing, I rolled my shoulders to relieve the tension. First things first, I wanted to make sure Sin was settled in before leaving.

I went poker-faced before entering my master bedroom.

Sin whirled away from my floor-to-ceiling window with awe transforming her face. "I'm jealous that you get to wake up to this beautiful view every morning, Core."

Sheer, boy-cut panties accentuated her voluptuous curves, and a body-hugging black tank top encased her tempting tits. She bit her lip as my eyes traveled from the top of her head down her curvy body.

"Unfortunately, I don't get to enjoy the view. I normally get in really late at night, and then I leave at the crack of dawn."

Damn. She was absolutely gorgeous with her hair cascading to her shoulders and her face freshly scrubbed. My length stirred, stiffening against my pants.

"Well, that's a fucking shame." She shifted from one foot to the other before swaying across the room. She climbed onto my king-size bed and slid under the sheets. "By the way, thank you for letting me stay here." She yawned. "And don't worry. I'm not moving in." She smiled impishly.

I shrugged. "I'm not worried about it." Walking over to the bed, I sat on the edge beside her.

Reclining back, she swallowed hard. "I feel stupid for saying this." She peered at me from under her long eyelashes. "But I was fucking scared shitless about being in my townhouse after—"

"Sin, stop torturing yourself. It's natural to feel that way." I handed her the glass in my hand. "Drink this. It's brandy."

Her long-fingered hands wrapped around the glass. Her gaze clouded, going distant. "I guess I wouldn't feel as creeped out about the intruder if something of value was actually stolen." Her face turned sullen. "Why would someone want an old ledger?" she muttered under her breath.

"What ledger?" I queried in a deliberately neutral voice.

She drew her brows together. "What?"

I stroked her hair. "You just mentioned something about a ledger."

She took a deep breath before letting it out slowly. "A couple weeks ago, I found a ledger stashed under a secret compartment in my father's ratty trunk. But nothing in the damn thing made a bit of sense. It was only random handwritten codes and numbers —essentially gibberish. The thing is—" she bit her bottom lip "—my father was an accountant, unglamorous and boring. So I can't figure out why he would even want to hide something like that."

Fuck. This shit was getting complicated. "Can't you ask your mother?"

Sin blinked her eyes rapidly. "Grace? Not a chance in hell. We don't talk."

She rubbed her brow as if to ward off a headache. Her pinched expression told me that matter was off-limits.

"Core, I'm sorry for snapping at you, but the topic of Grace isn't something I like to talk about." She sighed heavily. "Just put it this way, I cut her out of my life for a reason." One hand almost curled into a fist and then straightened. "Are you close to your mother?"

My muscles tensed slightly. "She died when I was young."

She gasped. "Oh God, I'm sorry."

There was a heaviness in the pit of my stomach. "It's not a subject I enjoy talking about."

She bowed her spine. "Believe me. I understand." She glanced away, then back.

Caressing her leg, I decided it would be better to change the subject quickly. "I'll have a couple of my investigators work on the break-in first thing today."

She inclined her head. "You don't have to do that. Talbot's got the case."

I pinned her in place with my steady gaze. "I would feel better if I conducted an independent investigation."

She took a large gulp of the brandy. "God, I feel absolutely nauseous about starting my collection all over again. All that work...gone." Her voice cracked.

I stroked her cheek. "You don't have to do it all by yourself. Whatever you need, I'll take care of it."

Placing her glass on the nightstand, Sin grabbed my face between her hands. "Thank you, Core." Her fingers shook. She jerked them away. She closed her eyes, her long, thick lashes fanning down on the glowing skin of her face.

"Sin," I demanded, lifting her face with my forefinger, "what's wrong?"

Within the expression on her gorgeous face, there was definitely something complicated.

She fluttered her eyelids half open, revealing the startling beauty of her eyes. "You don't know how much this means to me —you being here for me."

My heart jerked at the vulnerability and truth laid out in her words. I knew then that I would cut off my own arm before I'd ever let anyone harm her. "I always protect what I care for."

"Core, you're more of an enigma than I thought." She leaned in, tracing a finger along the light scar on my cheek and then farther up onto the jagged scar running across my eyebrow. "What are these from? A wicked bar fight?"

"Bad memories. Demons from my past that shaped the person I am today."

She curled her lips up into a slight smile. "Maybe someday you'll reveal the Core within."

"Maybe." My throat closed up. "But sometimes, the truth isn't so simple."

"We all have secrets we don't want to talk about because it hurts too much."

Drawing a breath, I released it before speaking, "Some more than others."

Her tongue darted out to touch her lips. "Someday, Core... we'll be able to let the demons go." Arching forward, she brushed her lips against mine before sliding under the sheets, closing her eyes.

I tucked them tightly around her soft, warm body. "Sleep tight, darling. I'll be back in a couple hours."

Her eyes snapped open. "Don't go." Her voice wavered.

Threading a hand through her hair, I murmured, "Okay, darling, I'll stay."

"Thank you."

I watched her nuzzle the pillow. Her eyelids drifted closed, and she promptly fell asleep. The bed dipped when I stood up. I headed to the bathroom, closing the door behind me. I groaned at the chaotic scene of Sin's personal items sprinkled around my master en-suite bath—bottles of body wash and lotion, her dress hanging next to her towel, her toothbrush next to mine. It reminded me of a happier time in my life with Maya. She had been my balance, my rock. I was willing to give up my criminal empire for her and my unborn child. One tragic moment and she'd been taken away, leaving me emotionally void. No woman could replace Maya in my heart. Until now.

A smirk rolled across my face. *Life is full of compromises*, I thought.

Then it dawned on me, the number of compromises I would be more than willing to make for this woman. Just the thought of her lying in my bed with those fucking barely there boy-cut panties displaying her luscious ass and her tight T-shirt outlining her voluptuous globes made my flesh go rock hard.

Turning on the shower, I adjusted the temperature to cold before stepping beneath the rain shower head, hoping the frigid water would get rid of my aching arousal. The jets beat against my body, but I was still at half-mast. As I soaped myself up, my hand lingered on my erection. I needed to stroke one out, or I'd end up turning her over and fucking the shit out of her.

Taking myself in my hand, I closed my eyes and tugged my cock. I thought about the taste of Sin's glistening sweet slit, my tongue licking her hard little nub, her hands tightly clutching my head against her weeping womanhood...

"Holy fuck," I hissed. I threw my head back, groaning as I ejaculated.

Quickly, I washed my body and hair, rinsing away the shampoo and soap. Snatching one of my luxurious towels, I dried myself off before putting on my lounge pants.

I left the bathroom to find Sin curled up in the middle of my king-size bed. She was snoring lightly. Turning out the light, I sat on the edge and the bed dipped. Then I lifted the covers and slid in beside her. As I edged my body closer, she mumbled something incoherent while inching her back until it fit snugly against my chest. I put my arm around her waist, and my legs pushed against the backs of her thighs, my nose nuzzling the back of her neck. I slowly dozed off. At that moment, I knew I had every-thing—Sin and Bigsby—and surprisingly, the anger was finally gone.

And one woman had unknowingly made it all happen—Sin.

❧ 10 ❧

CORE

MY PHONE VIBRATED on the nightstand, and I jerked straight up in bed. I grabbed it quickly, not wanting to wake Sin. The display told me it was Ram.

"Where the hell are you?"

Leave it to Ram not to beat around the damn bush.

"We've been waiting at the warehouse for hours."

Shit. I'd planned to call him, but I'd fallen asleep.

Now totally alert, I swung my legs over the bed and stood up. "Ram, give me a minute. I'm going down to my office."

Turning, I examined a fast-asleep Sin. I couldn't believe how peaceful and relaxed she appeared to be.

"Your office? Why can't you talk...?" Ram's voice trailed off. "Oh, fuck no. Don't tell me she's there, bro."

Silently padding out of my bedroom and closing the door behind me, I strode downstairs. I rubbed my forehead. "Of course she's here. I couldn't leave her in that fucked-up mess." Stepping into my soundproofed office, I slammed the door behind me.

"What mess?" Ram asked.

I paced back and forth. "Jeff's mess," I growled. My hand

tightened on the phone. "What the hell, Ram? Why didn't Max and Rocco stop him?"

There was a long pause.

"What are you talking about?" Ram asked calmly.

Jerking to a stop, I pounded my fist on the desk. "Sin's place, along with her collection, was trashed."

"What? Shit. Hold on. Let me get Max."

There was another long pause.

"I have Max here, and you're on speaker."

"What's the big emergency?" Max asked.

"What the fuck is wrong with you?" I barked. "I walked into her damn townhouse to find the whole place ripped to shreds. It was horrific. How could you let this happen?"

"We didn't let shit happen. In fact, we followed your instructions to a T," Max hissed. "You said hands off until we saw that damn ledger in Jeff's hand, and that was exactly what we did. Now you want to blame us because your brilliant plan turned into a clusterfuck? Come on, Core. This is bullshit."

My chest rose and fell with rapid breaths. "No, what's bullshit is I have to pick up the damn pieces because you and Rocco botched this job. Damn. I can't even trust you two to handle a fucking simple task." I knew my statement was irrational, but I didn't give a shit. Someone had to answer for this debacle.

"Core!" Ram snapped. "Are you even listening to yourself? What the fuck did you think Jeff was going to do when he broke in? Pussyfoot around and gently sift through her shit while searching for the ledger?"

"It was a damn break-in. That means shit gets broken." Max interrupted. "Did we think Jeff was going to fuck her place up? The answer is no. Obviously, you didn't either. Not that you gave a shit. All you cared about was getting that damn ledger. So, guess what, bro? You have the ledger and Jeff, too."

"Damn, you're right." I massaged the back of my neck. "We didn't know this shit was going to go down like that."

"And now that we have everything we need, what are your plans for Sin? Unless you're falling for her," Ram mused. "I hope not." He snorted.

I stiffened. "I'll be there in a few hours," I gritted out before throwing my cell onto the desk. I strode out of the office and back upstairs into the bedroom.

Closing the door behind me, I stood there for a good two minutes, wondering what the hell was wrong with me. She was supposed to be a means to an end. Nothing more. No attachments.

Shit, I never want to let her go.

All I wanted to do was go to her, wrap my arms around her, and protect her from the world.

Sin stirred. Her eyelids fluttered open, revealing the startling beauty of her almond-shaped hazel eyes. "What's wrong? You can't sleep?" she mumbled.

"I just called my team. I thought it'd be better for my guys to start on the trail while it's still fresh."

Sin smiled softly. "Come here, Core." She beckoned me with a little finger.

There were so many sides to Sin—sexy, rebellious, sassy, smart, vulnerable—and I wanted them all.

Marching over to the bed, I slipped between the sheets.

"You smell so good," she whispered before grabbing my hips.

Leaning in, she licked my lips and then plunged into my mouth with a persistent tongue. Her tongue slid around the tip of mine and then rubbed under it. I thought about her doing that to my cock, and I almost exploded.

Dammit!

I couldn't hold back any longer, not with her soft and pliant in my arms.

Groaning, I plundered, possessed, and nipped at her full lips before flipping her onto her back. I straddled her, one knee on each side of her waist. She gazed up at me, her eyes dilated. Her sensuous mouth curved into a smile.

I leaned down, biting her bottom lip. "I can't get enough of you."

She trailed her fingers across my chest. "I'm yours, Core. Fuck me."

I simply growled in response.

Wasting no time, I tugged off her tank and then her panties before sliding two fingers into her heat, stretching her open. She squeezed those fingers tightly, and I moaned just imagining how good she would feel around my cock.

"So beautiful," I murmured with approval as I slid down.

Molding her breasts with my hands, I sucked and bit her nipples until she was writhing beneath me, and then I journeyed down her body, pressing my mouth against her stomach, nibbling and kissing until all she seemed to want was to burst into flames.

Rising up on my elbows, I surveyed her hungrily before pushing her legs out a little. Now she was even more exposed and vulnerable before my gaze.

I cupped her wet sex. "Knees up to your stomach. Wide."

Giving me a salacious grin, she did what I commanded.

Damn. She follows instructions so well.

I pressed her knees outward, tipping her womanhood up in the air while gazing straight into her eyes. "This is how I always want you—open and ready for whatever I want and need from you." I slid my fingers between the wet folds of her heat. "This cunt is mine to do with as I please."

She arched up, wiggling closer, as my thumb circled and played with her clit.

"Whether it's with my cock or mouth, this pussy is all mine."

I stroked her smoldering wetness. She shivered as if she was on the verge of exploding. But I had no intention of letting her until she offered what I needed to hear—her soft request.

"Core," she whispered. "I...need—dammit. Please lick my pussy." Her breathing was ragged.

"My pleasure, Sinful."

My hands curled around her thighs, spreading her wider, and

my tongue thrust into her heat. That one lick sent her spiraling over the edge.

She wailed, "Core," like a prayer.

I pulled my head back, watching how her skin glowed and her eyes dilated, as my fingers continued to stretch her. "Louder, Sinful."

Her fingers gripped the sheets. "Dammit, Core."

"Louder," I demanded.

She was panting as her hips bucked wildly. My fingers pushed harder. She moaned louder when my finger found her clit again, playing with it mercilessly. She cried out and came again.

Panting and wasted, she lay boneless while I kicked off my pants and put on a condom. Getting back onto the bed, I hovered right above her, my weight on my knees between her thighs. Directing my head into position, I slipped in smoothly.

I couldn't take my eyes off her.

Her hazel eyes smoldered with intensity as my girth stretched her tight cunt.

With her nails desperately digging into my back, I grunted, "This cunt belongs to me," while fully seating myself with my balls bumping against her ass.

Feeling possessed, I grazed her lips and jaw. After pulling out, I sank back in with ruthless precision, hitting her G-spot. I wanted to fuck her until she was begging for air to breathe.

Her legs wrapped around my waist as I continued to hit her G-spot, making her legs quiver. I groaned when her slit sucked me in farther as I pumped harder. Her hips tilted up, and I adjusted my movements so, with each stroke, I brushed against her clit. The deeper I pumped, the louder she screamed. Her head thrashed back as I slid in and out. She wriggled beneath me. She was trembling, humming low. She stilled her hips so she could feel every inch of my pulsing manhood.

"I can't get enough of your cunt. I'm going to fuck you all night until you can't stand, darling," I growled into her ear, my cock forcing its way inside her again and again.

"Yes, yes, yes," she chanted, digging her nails into me like a wild woman.

I continued pumping, hard and controlled, making her mine with each stroke.

The entire time, we never looked away from each other. I couldn't help but love the way our bodies connected—stroke for stroke, touch for touch.

Sin was my equal.

Her breathing was fast and shallow with periods of whimpers intermixed. "Oh God, Core. Yes. Harder." She grabbed my head, pulling me closer, biting my lower lip. "Your gifted cock is mine."

Her words unleashed the fire within me. I let myself go, moving faster, pushing her into another orgasm. Arching, she screamed as her moist center spasmed around me. She collapsed right after, worn out and sweaty.

Pulling out of her body and flipping her onto her belly, I guided her up onto her knees. She mewled when I bit her neck. I brushed my lips over the tattoo of a guardian angel inked on her left shoulder and then on the large dove in flight on her right. Continuing on, I rained kisses along her spine.

Nudging her forward onto her hands, I massaged her buttocks. "You have the most beautiful ass," I rumbled. My fingers slid down the crack between her cheeks, touching her folds so intimately she gasped. "Fuck. You're so wet for me."

I slid my fingers through her wetness over and over until her hips squirmed uncontrollably. The air was sultry around us as my hands gripped her waist and I thrust into her smoothly.

Sin cried out with pleasure as one of my hands gripped her hair, with the other wrapped around her waist. I rocked my body into her. Our slick bodies were in perfect synchrony, with a strange magnetic energy encircling us.

She looked so comfortable against my skin.

"Don't stop," she whispered, shivering, as she gripped the bedsheets.

Growling, my fingers clutched the sides of her lush hips. I

reared back and pushed forward. Every inch of me was sheathed in her. Her body shuddered, her legs quivered, and her core pulsed.

"YOU AND ME, DARLING, FOR BETTER OR FOR WORSE," I STATED roughly, thrusting faster.

"Yes. For better or for worse, Core," she hissed.

"Fuck!" I cursed when she moved again.

"I'm going to come," she wailed.

"Not until I allow you."

My body slapped against hers ruthlessly. She rocked back into me, taking everything I had to give.

"Core, please."

My body burned for sweet release. "Now!" A strangled shout escaped my lips before I felt the orgasm ripping up my spine, tearing through my limbs.

Sin came so hard that she shouted my name at the top of her lungs. Her inner muscles contracted, milking me as both of us crested.

I kissed her on the shoulder before pulling her farther up on the bed. I clutched her body against mine. I wouldn't release her. I wouldn't let her go.

"Shit. That was fucking hot," I whispered against her lips.

"Hell yes, it was." She smiled even as she gasped for air.

I kissed her neck, her chin, her cheek. But it wasn't until I devoured her mouth with sweeping strokes of my tongue, slow and deep, that I realized I wanted Sin more than any woman I'd been with—even Maya.

~

THANK YOU FOR READING **TWISTED LIES 3!**

More Core and Sin goodness continues with **TWISTED LIES 4!**

And sign up for my newsletter to find out about new books...
www.sedonavenez.com/newsletter

ABOUT THE AUTHOR

USA TODAY BESTSELLING AUTHOR SEDONA VENEZ lives in New York City with her hot ex-military hubby—hooah—and their fur babies. She loves writing sizzling, sexy intricate stories about strong but broken characters who push limits, overcome their fears and risk it all for love.

Sedona loves to connect with readers!
www.sedonavenez.com

OTHER TITLES BY SEDONA VENEZ

Aliens!
Galaxy Alien Warriors - The Box Set
Beauty and the Alien Beast

Paranormal Romance
Shifter Alphas Furever Series
Claimed by Her Two Alphas
Claimed by Her Wolf
Claimed by Her Bear
Claimed by Her Dragon

Paranormal Romance
Credence Curse Series
Breaking the Storm
When Lightning Strikes
Taming the Beast
Reason to Love
Taming the Alpha Beast - The Box Set

Werewolves!
Wolf Elite Series

Operation Wolf: Gunner
Operation Wolf: Eli
Operation Wolf: Hunter
Wolf Elite - The Box Set

Bears!
Bear Elite Series
Operation Bear

Dark Romance
Dirty Secrets Series
Twisted Lies
Twisted Lies 2
Twisted Lies 3
Twisted Lies 4
Dirty Secrets - The Box Set

Contemporary Romance (MFM Ménage)
Standalone
Shameless Desires

Billionaire Romance
Standalone
Mr. Billionaire CEO

Urban Fantasy Romance
Magic Fire Collection

EXCERPT: TAMING THE BEAST

Want to sample a new series? Check out my Credence Curse books including this book, <u>Taming the Beast</u>.

I was stark naked—again. With huge ebony breasts swaying, ass jiggling, and designer stiletto-encased feet slapping against the dewy grass, I sauntered over to the center of the clearing.

Perching myself on top of the smooth boulder—or what I now lovingly called my rock of shame—I surveyed my recurring fixation.

My heart seemed to freeze and then pound. "Damn. You're such a beautiful kitty," I whispered.

Water cascaded off the tiger's magnificent reddish-rusty coat with narrow dark-brown stripes as he prowled out of the river toward me with rippling muscles. Its chest, throat, muzzle, and the insides of its limbs were creamy with a milky-colored area above the eyes that spread onto his cheeks.

When I extended my hand, he tilted his large head down, rubbing against it with a chuff-chuff sound.

"Hello, my big kitty. I'm happy to see you again, too," I answered his greeting. My digits trailed up to the white spot present on the back of its ear.

He nudged my hand away before circling me, his fur

caressing my bare legs while I admired the prominent ruff on his head and long tail ringed with noticeable dark bands.

Warmth radiated throughout my body as his fur deliciously tickled me.

"Every dream, you bring me here to watch you swim, and I still don't know why."

My mouth fell open when a deer pranced up to the river and drank from it, completely oblivious to the tiger's presence.

The tiger stilled, waited, and then pounced. The deer didn't even have a chance to run away before the tiger's big-as-saucers paws latched on to its hindquarters, bringing down the deer. The tiger gripped its neck, delivering a crushing bite to its prey. The deer stopped thrashing.

My fingers touched my parted lips before I closed them. "Holy shit."

This was a new addition to my nightly dreams. He'd never killed game before.

Wasting no time, the tiger dragged its dinner toward me, laying the carcass at my feet like an offering.

I gave him a weak half smile, trying desperately not to hurl at the sight of the dead deer. "Thank you, kitty, but it's a little . . . rare for me."

He flicked his tail, making a chuff-chuff sound, before his limbs quivered, shifted, and morphed into a very naked tall, muscular human.

"Elijah?" I stammered.

This couldn't be right. Animals didn't transform into humans, especially not into a man I was crushing on hard in real life.

"Yes, my Hope," he uttered in a dark, masculine voice.

Electricity sparked in my body as my eyes perused his mouthwatering splendor. His short, thick black hair had hints of gold, and his beard was well groomed. But it was his stunning but strange amber eyes with gold flecks that always made my stomach flip-flop, like a fish out of water. His eyes were the windows to his soul. They bored into me with an intensity that made my sex clench.

"Damn. Even in my dream . . . you're fucking splendid," I declared. My eyes trailed down his hard body to his engorged, perfect shaft standing at attention.

He clutched my face between his enormous, calloused hands. "Eyes up here, darling." His face dissolved into an exquisite grin. "Unless you're finally ready to get on all fours for your big kitty?" His hands dropped away and grabbed me around the waist, yanking me against his naked body.

"My, you're such a dirty pussycat, and I love it." I licked his bottom lip.

"So that's a yes." It was a statement, not a question.

"Baby, I'll do whatever you want . . . however you want. But only if you promise to lick all my cream, like a good kitty."

We stared at each other with my legs straddling one of his rock-solid thighs.

"There's nothing good about me, darling, but I can promise to lick you to the very last drop." His voice was thick with emotion. "Just say when, my beautiful mate."

EXCERPT: CLAIMED BY HER TWO ALPHAS

Want to sample a new series? Check out my Shifter Alphas Furever books including this book, <u>Claimed by Her Two Alphas</u>.

In the two weeks since that conversation with Peyton, one snippet of that bizarre conversation kept running through my head. These guys were looking for their perfect *mate*. Not mates, plural. Not one guy wanting one and the other guy wanting... something else. Both guys were looking for the same thing, and according to Alex, that thing was me. But I was only one woman and even if I'd gotten past the weirdness of two guys wanting to share one blind date, I still hadn't wrapped my head around how I could be the perfect mate for both of them.

Yet here I was, trying to figure out how I was going to find not just one, but two blind dates in a crowded bar. I should have backed out.

No. You shouldn't have. It's not going to kill you to do this. If it back-fires, you can tell Peyton "I told you so."

At least I should have figured out some way to recognize these guys, like carrying a rose or wearing a bow in my hair. Or maybe a name tag, so instead of standing in the crowd turning in useless circles, I could find these guys. I made another sweep of the room.

You're overthinking...just take a breath and let go.

I closed my eyes, wavering slightly in my heels, did my best imitation of someone poised and collected, and concentrated on my breathing. Then I opened my eyes. The crowd parted and there he was. Or there *some* guy was, some really handsome guy.

He was sitting at the bar, and he was looking right at me. For a split second I thought I'd made him up, or maybe I'd hallucinated him out of desperation. Even sitting down, he was big and broad-shouldered, taking up more physical space than anyone around him. Or maybe he just looked like he was. He should have been imposing, scary, but he radiated an all-American boy kind of feel, the hunky guy-next-door who helped you with your groceries or changed the flat on your car. *A nice, safe guy.*

Until I got to his eyes. Blue. Even in the dim light of the bar, I could tell they were blue. The all-American hunk had just turned the tiniest bit dangerous. There was a fire in those eyes that woke up something deep and primal, something I'd thought didn't exist in me. Or at least I'd never experienced it. I wouldn't go as far as calling it love at first sight; lust at first sight, maybe. Whatever it was, it was pretty amazing.

I really wanted to take a step forward, but I was rooted in place. His eyes held mine, never looking away, and it was like a magnet, drawing me closer. Something held me back though.

But wait...what about my date? Just because this guy likes looking at me...and I like looking at him...

I turned away, the act of breaking away from his gaze doing nothing to lessen the heat that had built up inside me. I was supposed to be here looking for my mystery men, not falling for the first guy who caught my eye.

Turn around...what if it's him?

That thought came out of the blue. And for once, I listened to the voice in my head and did a slow turn. The guy was smiling at me, and something inside me simultaneously clenched and loosened up. It was a physical sensation, a thud deep and low, and I took a step back, shocked by my body's reaction.

When he stood, I saw just how tall he was, well over six feet. He cut easily through the crowd toward me with a grace that belied his size. He stopped just in front of me, and I looked up into those piercing blue eyes.

"Hi, Sadie. I'm Dane. Dane Hastings."

I stared. Just plain unattractively, open-mouthed, deer-in-headlights stared at this amazing specimen, who'd just told me he was one half of my blind date. Saints preserve me, maybe I'd gotten lucky. Then it hit me.

Where the hell was the other guy?